The Desired Effect

The Desired Effect

ANDREW GIMSON

CHAPMANS

1991

Chapmans Publishers Ltd
141–143 Drury Lane
London WC2B 5TB

BRITISH LIBRARY CATALOGUING IN PUBLICATION DATA

Gimson, Andrew
The desired effect.
I. Title
823.914[F]

ISBN 1-85592-014-X

First published by Chapmans 1991
Copyright © 1991 by Andrew Gimson

Photoset by Rowland Phototypesetting Ltd, Bury St Edmunds, Suffolk
Printed and bound in Great Britain by
Bookcraft (Bath) Ltd

One

It was such a nuisance David could not be there. Belinda had invited several of his friends to welcome him home, and, most likely, to hear an announcement. Now she was a man short.

She did not want to ask anyone who had shown signs of falling in love with her. It would be unfair to raise hopes. Nor did she wish to throw away months of self-restraint by giving David cause for jealousy just before he returned. She wished she could cancel this wretched dinner, but it was too late for that.

Until February she might have fallen back on Hamish Stuart. The trouble with him was that he could be a bore about politics – indeed about any subject – but he was an old friend of David's, and usually available until he took the reckless step of getting engaged. Belinda had invited the pair of them, as she wanted to see what his fiancée, Ann-Louise, was like.

Two other couples were coming. Eight to dine was enough: ten would be cramped in her flat. The living-room was shaped in an L, round a kitchen taken out of one corner of the original room, and her dining-table fitted tightly into the shorter part of the L.

So who should be the seventh guest, the man to balance her? Perhaps she had met everyone she ever would, and was doomed to circulate in the same set, without any innovation, until she died.

5

A possibility occurred to her, so youthful she could treat him as safe. Before Christmas she had been to spend a weekend in Wales, at the house of some people called Eliot. They had a young man staying, a potter. The Eliot daughter, Corinna, who had been about to go to Australia, knew him from art college.

Belinda was amused by him. He was attractive, and had the good manners or insolence not to gawk at her beauty, which reduced most men of his age to gaucheness.

They joked with each other: she was fond of jokes, not only for themselves, or because she was told she had a delightful laugh, but because they were a way of being friends while keeping a distance. Before leaving the Eliots', she asked him where she could find his studio, in case she wanted to buy some of his pots. He wrote down his name, telephone number and an address in Ealing.

The justification for asking him was that he would diversify a dinner-party where the others were on their best, upper-middle-class behaviour.

Tom Coleman had to be fetched when she rang.

'Hello?'

'Tom, it's Belinda Gould. We met at the Eliots'.'

'Oh yes.'

'It's frightfully short notice, but I'm having some people to dinner tonight and wondered if you might like to come?' No reply. 'Or whether you're offended that you've only been asked to fill in for someone else at the last moment?'

'I'll come if you promise not to tell anyone I'm a substitute,' he said, sounding amused.

'They won't suspect a thing.' She gave him the address of her flat – 'It's only five minutes from Hammersmith tube' – and suggested he come about 8.30. After she had rung off, she wondered what he would wear. All weekend he had been in a sweater and a pair of jeans, except on Saturday night, when the rest of the men had worn suits and he put on a different sweater.

Early in the evening she came home from work, finished

6

the cooking (mostly done last night), checked that everything down to the coffee cups was ready, had a bath and dressed. To amuse herself she put on some of the black silk underwear David had given her. He had looked so grave when he first saw her wearing it that she could not help giggling; feared he was hurt; but no, he said her *joie de vivre* attracted him. It seemed to Belinda that the suspender belt attracted him more. How ludicrous the outfit was. She hid it under a little black dress and looked at herself in the mirror.

Her neck showed to such advantage when her blonde hair was lifted behind her ears that David would ask her to put it up, or gather it in his hands and stand at arm's length looking at her. Or he would hold her before the mirror, to get a more distant view. 'But that is a mere reflection,' he would say. Then he would bury his face in her neck, know she was excited, kiss her passionately.

He also enjoyed kissing her nipples. There were elements of repetition in his approach. Unfair of her to think that, but they had been together years.

Tonight she left her hair down.

Tom arrived first: her flat was on the first floor and had no remote-control gadget for opening the front door, so she went downstairs to let him in.

When she took his coat, she saw to her surprise that he was wearing a suit, old and black with narrow lapels. His shoulders were not broad enough for the jacket; the dark blue shirt was crumpled and frayed, and open at the neck. The way he stood suggested lazy force, as if he could not be bothered to exert himself.

'What will you have to drink?' she asked. He was examining pictures and ornaments. 'I'm afraid my taste must seem rather conventional,' she added.

'Yes,' he replied, when she had expected a denial. Parts of the scheme were quite daring. The marble fireplace was ornate for so small a room. To one side of it she had hung a drawing of a female nude, taken from Rodin's sculpture

7

of a Danaid. The normal compliment was: 'Is this you?'

'I'd forgotten how modern you are,' she said.

'My partner's into Victorian patterns. They sell.'

His partner? At the pottery, of course. He'd mentioned him before.

'Gin? Whisky? Wine?' she found herself asking. God she sounded stilted.

'Whisky thanks. The same amount of water. No ice.'

He stood still, reading the first page of a book. His self-possession annoyed her. He looked about ten years old. It was usually the task of putting young men at their ease that helped her to feel at ease herself.

She put his drink on the mantelpiece, just next to him.

'Tell me what you've been doing,' she said, wanting to get him out of the book.

'Why do you look so upset?'

The doorbell went before she could ask what he meant by that piece of nonsense.

'Tom, let me introduce you to Jenny and Matthew Scott-Woodhouse.'

Matthew wore a double-breasted suit in grey flannel, a striped, immaculately laundered shirt and a red silk tie. He started a story about going out last Saturday to shoot pigeons with the farmer who lived next to their weekend cottage in Dorset. Jenny asked Tom if he shot. She was wearing a tartan dress and had a jaw which made her look like a donkey. He said no, he didn't shoot.

Hamish and Ann-Louise arrived. Belinda tried to swallow the uncharitable thought that the girl was the right age to be a bimbo, but not pretty enough. She was thin, and the pallor of her face against her short dark hair made her look unhealthy. She had dressed as though for a disco, in purple Lycra skirt and sleeveless white top. Hamish's own appearance acquired, in her company, a certain interest, as if he made a fashion statement by being a drabber version of Matthew.

Once the latter had shown he was a true countryman, no

8

snob who would only shoot with nobs, the talk turned to shooting with nobs, though you didn't mention who they were. You just said: 'When we were at Nobden in November.'

James and Celia Eyre were introduced. She wore a brown suit; James the same as Matthew and Hamish, between the two of them for slickness. Belinda parried their inquiries about David and poured them drinks. Refills for the others. Jenny related an episode in Perthshire. All the talk was done properly. These were professional people who were working hard and getting on, and brought to their social life the same application, the same aptitude for seeing how to go about things, as they used in their careers.

Matthew was describing an incompetent member of the party with whom he went stalking, who shot a stag in the rump, which was about as far as you could get from the heart. Celia Eyre asked whether Tom had a card. She needed a wedding present for her friend Natasha. Getting a pot made by Tom would, she said, be so much more interesting than looking at their list at the General Trading Company and ordering a couple of cut-glass tumblers. She hated cut-glass tumblers.

Belinda went to the kitchen, separated by an arrangement of shelves and cupboards from the rest of the room. She wished they hadn't talked so much about shooting. Faults she usually overlooked became excruciating when she tried to imagine how these people, all trying to be slightly grander than they were, would look to Tom. He must hold the game 'let's play landed gentry' in contempt.

'Come and sit down,' she said.

'But where's David?' Matthew asked. 'I thought we were waiting for David. Jenny was quite excited on the way here, she said we were going to celebrate.'

'He rang at lunchtime. He's sorry, he's stuck in Zimbabwe. Something to do with the RAF.'

'I'm the substitute,' Tom said.

She got everyone placed, with Hamish on her right and

Tom on her left. The first course was a delicious terrine made of fish and egg, with anchovies and olives on top. It was applauded, except by Tom, who was absorbed in a conversation with Jenny.

'We are so looking forward to the wedding,' she said.

He raised his glass.

'Quite right,' Jenny went on. 'I drink to them too. Don't tell Belinda I told you, because I promised David I wouldn't, but they got engaged the night he went away. He's frightfully good news for her. She's thirty-four.'

Tom did not need to ask what difference that made, as a little wine had rendered Jenny confidential.

'She's thirty-four and she's still beautiful!'

'Wouldn't that mean she could marry someone else?' he asked.

'Spoilt for choice! So while any sensible woman settles' – she glanced at Matthew and was reassured to see he was making a map of a grouse moor out of some cutlery – 'for what she can get, she's been waiting to fall in love! It's driven us all round the bend, not least David! I'm his cousin, so I know.'

'Poor bloke,' Tom said.

'And she's terrified of losing her looks. The one thing people envy her for has become the most crushing burden. Besides, looks like hers so often end up attracting the wrong kind of chap.'

It was, he supposed, an ingenious way for Jenny to cope with her ugliness.

'Not to mention children,' she added. 'We've a boy and a girl, and that can be hard to bear if you're thirty-four and childless.'

'I'd no idea she was in such a tragic state,' Tom said.

'Not tragic. She's sorted it out.'

Belinda had Hamish's help to clear the plates and bring on the main dish, boeuf bourguignon. The conversation grew more general. She saw Tom listening as though to a group of lunatics, and wanted to whisper in his ear that she too could hear their oddity.

Hamish was trying to become an MP. He had fought a hopeless seat in Lancashire last time, was looking now for a safe one. The others started to ask him the questions they would put if they were on the selection committee.

Matthew said that with his farming expertise (he earned his living as a merchant banker but knew people who farmed) the selection committee would probably expect him to ask something about the pig quota, or the Common Agricultural Policy, but to be honest, and he didn't want this to be taken the wrong way, what really interested him was the candidate's wife.

'That's ridiculous, Matthew,' Belinda said. 'It's not the wife who's going to represent the constituency in Parliament –'

'Somebody once claimed if you want to know what a man's like, you should look at the mental health of his wife,' James interjected.

'Exactly,' Matthew said. 'A man's choice of wife says a lot about him. I like to think I would have no trouble getting a seat, once the selection committee met Jenny' – he smiled at her – 'and besides, it's quite likely the wife who will stay in the constituency and do a lot of the slog.'

'I've been with Hamish to several selection meetings,' Ann-Louise said. 'They want to check, first that I'm going to live in the constituency, second that I shan't have a career of my own, third that any time one of the branches wants to have a wine and cheese party, and Hamish is stuck at Westminster, I'll come as his representative.'

'Dearest, I don't think it would be as bad as all that. In practice the agent would do most of the work. We'd just have to attend some of the weekend functions.'

'Like half a dozen, plus a couple of surgeries for you. When the House is sitting I'll hardly see you.' This plaintive note did not impress Belinda.

'Why do you want to be a Member of Parliament?' Tom enquired.

'I wish I knew. People say it's a form of insanity, and Ann-Louise hates the idea.'

'It's an addiction,' Ann-Louise explained. 'I can't cure him of it. He started at St Andrews in the Conservative Association. Then he became a local councillor in Kensington. Then he fought that seat. Then he met me, and now we're looking for a safe seat. The last one to come up, he reached the last four. The worst of it is I lost it for him.'

'Darling, I honestly don't think you did.'

'Well, that was what your friend of a friend on the committee said. "It seemed to us that your fiancée had a mind of her own" was how he put it.'

'Look,' James said, 'I've known Hamish since we were at university. With the exception of himself, the people who joined the Conservatives were a bunch of humourless little creeps who went around licking the arses of the ministers who came up to speak. What we've got to do is persuade Hamish not to ruin himself, and make Ann-Louise's life a misery, by associating with them.'

'But if everyone thought that,' Tom said, 'the country would be left in the hands of humourless little creeps.'

'Quite right,' Belinda agreed. 'There are far too many of those in power already. Hamish has got to represent us.'

'As I was saying only the other day, to a dining club which asked me to address them,' the prospective MP began, 'when bad men combine, the good must associate; else they will fall, one by one, an unpitied sacrifice in a contemptible struggle.'

'How very true,' Belinda said, thinking they could do without the rest of the speech.

'That bit's by Burke. What I myself went on –'

'Maybe Belinda should stand for Parliament,' Tom interrupted. For a moment she caught his eye.

'There's no reason why not,' Hamish replied. 'We need

more women. What I went on to discuss, after I'd given them that bit of Burke –'

'The women will keep out the women,' Ann-Louise said. 'There are plenty of women on the selection committees but they won't choose one of themselves.'

'Will anyone have some more?' Belinda asked for form's sake, before she removed the casserole.

'Yes, please,' Tom said. Several people had already said it was delicious (which was true), but they couldn't (which was false). They saw Tom eat a second helping as large as the first. Belinda liked feeding a boy who needed it. It made a change from proving you could cook a reasonably sophisticated boeuf bourguignon.

She sent the bottle round the table. The self-restraint of those who stuck to mineral water displeased her. Ann-Louise, for example, who covered the top of her wine glass with her hand.

'Won't you have a drop?'

'No, thanks. I've given up for Lent.'

This idea of giving up for Lent was spreading. People did it because they thought it was good for their health. Belinda usually drank almost nothing at her own parties. The abandonment of her rule exhilarated her. Would it be unkind to consider Ann-Louise sour?

Tom finished his second plateful with amazing speed and Hamish again helped her to clear. They were the two best placed to get out.

Chocolate mousse flavoured with brandy. A bowl of fruit. Coffee. The party was going so well they did not move from the table. She lay back, drawing on a cigarette, enjoying the two or three conversations going on at once. Not all her guests were so health-conscious as to have given up smoking, though she herself was trying to cut down. She saw to it that they had wine. She wouldn't offer liqueurs, that would be excessive. Hamish was explaining a political point to her. He wanted to elucidate something he told the dining club. She slipped off her shoes and put her feet on the edge of

Tom's chair. By tilting back her own, and twisting her body to the right, she could still talk to Hamish. She ended up rather close to him.

'You're bound to find a seat. You're so well-qualified,' she said.

'I'm worried that it's not fair on Ann-Louise. She hasn't taken to the life.'

'She's very lucky to be marrying you.' Why did she say these things? She should stop herself. She hardly knew Ann-Louise, but supposed she wanted everything to go well for her. Hamish was dependable, not a show-off like Matthew, and stood to inherit a house in Gloucestershire. He was an excellent solution to Ann-Louise's problem of unmarried, would-be motherhood – if that was Ann-Louise's problem. The non-bimbo was only just out of university. Belinda concentrated on talking to Hamish, intending, in a perverse way, to stop Tom ignoring her.

'And another thing,' Hamish was saying, his fiancée safely absorbed in talk on the other side of the table. 'She's getting very interested in Roman Catholicism. I think she might convert, and my mother can't bear Romans. She says the converts are the worst. They get so intolerant and insist on bringing up the children their way. You aren't going over yourself, are you?'

'Oh no,' she assured him. 'I'm just the usual kind of Anglican who doesn't go to church. I go when I'm at home.'

'Quite right. One ought to go in the country. The parishes are being amalgamated because too few of us go to church.'

She half turned to Tom. He had stopped talking to the people on his left and was taking a swig of wine. He might be looking at her stockinged feet on his chair. Her toes almost touched him. She tried to think of something to say.

'Do you go to church?' she asked.

'I'm an atheist.'

'Oh! And what are your family?'

'We're Jewish. My parents are secular.'

'Jesus was a Jew,' Hamish said. He could deliver any remark as if it were original.

'I like Jesus,' Tom said to her, not Hamish. 'He upset people.' She had his attention and was not sure she wanted it. His manner said: 'Do you expect me to be impressed?' The sight of her legs stretched out, her dress tight about her thighs, the light shimmering on her stockings, should have produced a more generous reaction. She gathered her hair behind her head. Tom was so ill-mannered. He had shifted so that his leg pushed against her toe. Hamish was making a theological point.

There was a disturbance on the other side of the table. James and Celia were getting ready to leave. Belinda had hardly exchanged a word with Celia all evening. Nor had she spoken to James, who used to be so witty, and had once, just after she met David, made a pass at her. He kept Celia happy. It was harder and harder to stay in touch with people. Life from now on would be the process of losing contact. Tom's leg was still against her, but as though she were a bump on the chair.

'We must make a move,' James said.

'Don't all go,' she urged. The dinner had been a success. It was midnight: people who worked in the City didn't generally stay later. But she hoped they wouldn't all rush off at once.

'James and I mustn't break up the party,' Celia said. Belinda got up to fetch their coats from her bedroom. She heard James ask if they could give a lift 'anywhere on the way to Pimlico'.

'I'm too far north,' Tom said. So he worked in Ealing but lived somewhere north of a line between Hammersmith and Pimlico. She came back in with James and Celia's coats. Everyone was standing up. She felt unbearably nervous.

'Mind you let us know the minute David gets back,' Jenny said. 'Matthew and I are simply dying to see the two of you together. Maybe we can give you a lift, Tom? Where exactly do you live?'

15

'Don't all go,' Belinda repeated.

'Notting Hill Gate,' Tom said.

'We're in St John's Wood. We can easily drop you off,' Matthew assured him.

'Let's stay a few minutes longer,' Ann-Louise said to Hamish. 'You're not going, are you, Tom?'

'Perhaps I'll stay.'

So the three of them stayed. Thank God Ann-Louise hadn't had time to acquire sensible habits about parties.

Belinda poured the dregs of some wine. Everyone told her not to open another bottle. The talk faltered. She feared Tom would go with the others; feared he would stay. He asked for some whisky. She gave it to him.

Nobody accepted her suggestion that she make more coffee. Hamish yawned. She was sitting away from Tom now. The rule she imposed on herself was that all encouragement must be ambiguous.

Her ally, Ann-Louise, fended off silence by asking the whereabouts of Tom's studio. It was ground that should have been covered at the start of the evening. Tom's replies were monosyllabic. The flat felt cold. Her central heating must have gone off.

'I don't know about you lot,' Hamish said, 'but I suddenly feel flat out. I really think we ought to make tracks, darling. You must let us drop you, Tom.'

The three of them stood up. Belinda went to get their coats. She was thankful: heaven knows what would have happened if he'd stayed. She might have yielded to a passing infatuation, and regretted it.

She came back along the corridor which led from her bedroom, at the back of the house, to the living-room at the front. A second bedroom and the bathroom lay between. Her guests were in the corridor, waiting by the door onto the landing, saving her from herself. She felt utterly in need of him. She wanted them all to go so she could stop being self-possessed.

He took his coat from her, a black garment as shabby as

his suit, and held it against himself, his hands clasped in front, while Ann-Louise and Hamish put theirs on. She did not look at him. He was a blur in the corner of her eye.

'Thank you very much,' Ann-Louise said. 'I'm glad we've met.'

Hamish opened the door. 'It really was splendid,' he said. 'See you both in Gloucestershire if not before.' She had accepted an invitation for her and David to visit Hamish's mother's house next weekend.

'Can I stay to finish my whisky?'

The simplicity of Tom's question was breath-taking. He didn't say: 'Actually, I wonder, could I possibly stay a minute or two, just to finish my whisky?'

'Yes,' she managed to reply. She had never seen Hamish so startled. The enormity of their behaviour stunned him. He looked from Belinda, upon whom he had always depended, to 'the young whippersnapper' (as he put it in the car on the way home) 'who just stood there cool as a cucumber'.

Ann-Louise had gone out. 'Good night,' Hamish said, and followed. The door, flimsy but quite opaque, closed behind them. Tom let his coat fall to the floor. Without a word, he kissed her.

The relief of that embrace! All her loneliness seemed to flood from her. She stood a long moment against him, broke free and led him into the living-room. For the first time that evening he moved clumsily, almost treading on her. She felt him tremble.

'Where's your bathroom?' he asked. Nerves: such a diuretic. He went back down the corridor, found it beyond the door onto the landing. She lit the gas fire in her marble fireplace. When he came back, she went. How romantic.

He was sitting on the sofa, one leg crossed over the other, when she returned. She brought his drink from the dining-table, sat on the edge of the sofa, passed it to him. He took a sip.

'Do you want some?'

She shook her head. He put it to one side, drew her to him. His kisses became almost painful.

'You're wonderful,' he said. She sighed and kissed him again. He had praised her: the natural order was restored.

The sofa was small, so it would fit into the flat. Tom must have pushed too hard with his legs. It slid backwards into some dining-chairs and they fell onto the carpet, rolling over before the fire until she sat astride him.

'What sexy underwear!' he said, running his hands over her.

'How old are you?' she asked.

'Guess.'

'Twenty-seven.'

'Twenty-four. How old are you?'

'How old do you think?'

'Twenty-seven, too.'

'Thirty-four.'

Prolonged kissing, during which he tried and failed to remove her dress.

'Wait,' she said, standing up. She brushed herself down, took some mineral water, perched on the sofa. He sat cross-legged on the floor, watching her.

'I must have drunk much too much,' she said. 'You ought to go. What would your girlfriend say?'

'I haven't got one.'

'I do. Boyfriend, I mean. We're going to get married and live happily ever after.'

'How unbearable.'

'Come and sit with me, if you'll be good.'

'I'll be good.'

'Why did you call me upset?' she asked once he was sitting beside her.

'You aren't now.' He reached out to stroke the side of her face. It was impossible to tell who was more aroused by the other's passion. They ended up with his head thrown back against the sofa, hers resting against his chest while he

18

stroked her hair. Her wrists were drawn up tight together, as if in self-defence.

'Why?' she repeated.

'Can't we go to bed?'

'You don't know how this matters to me.' However much she hoped to talk to others, she found that when they met she could not confess her dissatisfaction. But Tom had seen it. If he knew, she could tell him.

'I guessed,' he said. 'It was like looking at a hand of cards and seeing how it might play.'

'I don't like being compared to a game.'

'What about poker?' he laughed, with excessive vulgarity; went on stroking. She moved against him. 'I don't mean I was playing you,' he said. 'I just thought I understood you. I expect I was completely wrong.'

'What did you understand?'

'You looked as if you'd got mixed up with the wrong kind of people. People who think life's fine provided you've got an old rectory.'

'I wouldn't mind one.'

'What gets me is they take it all so seriously. They won't do anything which doesn't help them get an old rectory.'

'And me?'

'They'd like you as well, to go with the house.'

'I was attempting to have a serious conversation. What makes you think I'm not one of them?'

'Sleeping with me wouldn't help you get an old rectory.'

'What a curious way of putting it.'

'Haven't you ever treated anything as a joke?'

'Like what?'

'Like sleeping with someone.'

'Tom Coleman, the joke in bed.'

'No!'

'Just a joke.'

'I'd like the chance to clear my name.'

'You men get so worked up about proving things. I just like being with someone.'

'Plain girl, plain tastes.'

'Exactly.'

'You're not plain, you're amazing.'

Silence. He wondered after a while if she had gone to sleep, so steady was her breathing; smoothed her dress and felt his desire return.

She mumbled something he could not hear and pushed herself upright, so she was sitting next to him again on the sofa. He fell sideways and she held him against her. She saw he was expecting she would now yield.

'It's time you went home,' she said.

'What?'

'It's far too soon.'

'When your fiancé turns up it'll be much too late.' He resumed his attack on her dress.

The words she had mumbled, 'I think I love you,' were too embarrassing to say out loud.

'Go home,' she told him.

Two

David Cheney at length got back from Zimbabwe, where he had been seconded to the British team instructing 'native troops', as he called them. He was an officer in the Life Guards. One of his ambitions was to command the regiment, but since it wasn't done to show keenness, Belinda was the only person in whom he had confided. She would, he assured her, make an excellent commanding officer's wife.

He took life seriously, and was at first so annoyed by his brother officers' pretence that it was all a moderately amusing waste of time, that he wondered if he should transfer somewhere like the Paras. Then he could be a professional soldier without amateur camouflage.

Family tradition would not have been sufficient to hold him loyal to the Life Guards, though once the Cheneys had withdrawn from the manufacture of soap, that was the regiment they tended to join. His motive was love of horses. The Life Guards knew about horses, and were indulgent to officers who wanted time to hunt or go racing. He met Belinda at Ascot. He detested the social side of the place but went there to see a horse.

The girl wore an outlandish hat (her picture was in the next day's papers) and was with a youth who was in public relations, and wanted to drink champagne and stare at people. She was interested in the races, and in her excitement asked David, who looked knowledgeable and was standing next to her, a question. He lent her his field glasses.

The afternoon worked out strangely. She chatted him up. He was heavy going, because he thought she looked flashy, maybe tipsy too, and the race he wanted to see was run while she was at her most inquisitive. Someone came up and said he was sorry David's horse hadn't done better. Belinda was amazed he had not mentioned his ownership. David said he only had one leg of the beast. She was aghast that she had 'monopolized his binocs' during the race.

Her escort came back. David saw Belinda was beautiful, had liked it when she put her hand on his arm and stood on tiptoe to see better; but he grew more reticent as a result. If she would open a conversation with him, she might talk to anyone, and she was the kind of girl who would need entertaining. Besides, he was suspicious of her eagerness to know about racing.

But she was in a bit of a fix. The youth with her looked totally unfit to drive, yet wanted to leave before the last race 'to get ahead of the traffic'.

'I'd much rather stay,' she said. David had to credit her for not giving him a beseeching look.

'We're leaving,' the youth repeated. 'We've seen everyone.'

'If you need a lift to London, I'll be driving up later,' David offered.

'I don't believe we've been introduced,' the youth said, his tone a parody of good manners.

'Would you come over here?' David said, taking his arm. 'Excuse us.'

Belinda never knew what he said to her escort. More than anything, she felt ashamed to have come to Ascot with such a man. Presumably David was embarrassed on her behalf, or thought you shouldn't have arguments in front of women. He was extraordinary. She could not think of another man who would have dealt with the situation like that, in a voice so devoid of doubt as to stop any attempt at resistance.

David was not very tall and, she later discovered, was starving himself in preparation for a ride. On the other hand, he looked alarmingly fit.

'I'm sorry,' she said, when he returned alone, his grimness giving way to a polite smile on seeing her.

'You've no reason to be.'

'First I take your binocs and then I make you deal with that awful boy. I'd no idea he was so ghastly.'

'Not everyone is improved by drink.' He insisted she say no more about it. She was relieved. On the way back to London, she tried to get him to tell her about the army. This, he thought, was the same trick as she used about racing.

'Nobody's interested in the army,' he said.

'But I am. I like hearing what people do.' He realized he might have been unduly suspicious. The girl might suffer from indiscriminate curiosity. He could not see her real ailment was shyness, hidden by a screen of questions.

'What do you do?' he asked.

'Oh, nothing that would interest you.'

'You're as bad as me,' he said, and they both laughed.

'Isn't it horrible having to ask people what they do?' she confided.

'I suppose it is,' he said, in such a detached way as to suggest he had no idea what she was talking about. By the end of the journey, he had made himself as remote as before. She felt sorry for him. If he was like this now, he would be weird in a few years' time. He needed teasing.

She sent a postcard of thanks to Hyde Park Barracks, with her address and telephone number; was mildly piqued to hear nothing until two months later, when he wanted a partner for some regimental festivity. On this occasion, which she dreaded, and for which she spent weeks wondering what to wear (How smart should one be for something called a 'street party'?), she shone. The officers were charmed by her. She liked the ease of their welcome: they made her feel at home, something so unexpected in that formal setting as to be delightful. They seemed more relaxed, more contemporary than her partner. Seated by the commanding officer, she let herself be coaxed into an innocent-wanton conversation. This pleased both him and his wife. Only David was angry. On the way home in a taxi, sitting in the other corner to herself, he apologized for the 'intolerable behaviour' she had encountered.

'But they were sweet,' she said sweetly. 'They said I'd find you're a superb rider.'

'They treated you as though you were getting married to me.'

'Is that such an insult?'

'It's damn presumption. Totally unfair on you. As for Andrew!' Words failed him when he thought of the way another officer tried to ingratiate himself with Belinda. David had to put his arm round her when he thought how Andrew had behaved.

'You can't have it both ways. Either I was with you or I wasn't.'

To answer this question, David found it essential to kiss her, then tell the driver to go to his flat rather than hers. On arrival, she refused to come in. He was huffy. She decided it was only fair to invite him to her parents' house in Yorkshire for the following weekend. The interesting fact that unlike any of her other friends, he owned racehorses, made her try all the harder to see the good in him.

Her father shuddered at the intenseness of his daughter's new friend, but outwardly accepted him. Her mother fell in love with David, much preferring him to the estate agent Belinda had brought home last time.

It is almost impossible for those unworried by such things to know with what charm the word 'Eton' may fall upon the ear. Laetitia Gould (Letty to her friends) was infinitely susceptible to the sound, especially as she had endured several disappointments before David came to stay. The eldest of her three daughters, Charlotte, had been infected by the proletarianism of the 1960s. She took herself away from boarding school and enrolled at the technical college in the local town, where she cohabited with a lorry driver called Barry Pugg, acquiring a Yorkshire accent and failing her exams. After the birth of their second child, she and Barry got married at a registry office and she started keeping accounts for him, as he had acquired several trucks. Although Mrs Gould's confident fear, that Barry would up and leave Charlotte and the children penniless, had not been realized (indeed, Pugg Transport International showed signs of prospering), it was not the outcome one would have wished. Mr Gould's drinking sessions with Barry did nothing to soften the blow.

Her second daughter, Sophie, started well. She married a gentleman farmer who had a fine Georgian house, where he entertained the whole of his wife's family, including the Puggs. Neither Mr Gould nor Barry Pugg liked him, and Belinda loathed him for an attempt he had made on her when she was fifteen, but Mrs Gould regarded him as a highly suitable match. Her own life had been spent trying to maintain a genteel existence on an inadequate income, a struggle to which her parents had devoted themselves entirely, but which Henry, her husband, had given up. He was the son of a colonial bishop, had been educated at an obscure school but won a classical scholarship to Oxford, later qualifying as a solicitor.

In his youth, he not only had a well-bred manner but was said to be a gifted lawyer. Yet he used her desire to move to the country as an excuse to settle down as a country lawyer near Darlington. The more ambitious she was on his behalf, the less capable he became of social or professional effort. His relish for Pugg's company was in her opinion part of a tragic coarsening. He even refused an invitation to shoot, on the childish pretext that he could not bear the thought of a day in the company of the baronet who issued it. This was a bitter blow, wasting many years of charitable work during which Mrs Gould had got to know Lady Erpingham, the baronet's wife.

Sophie's marriage, which was childless, lasted three years. She grew tired of the farmer's philandering, took up with an American and went to Chicago.

Belinda was the last hope. Mrs Gould used an unexpected legacy to send her to an excellent school in the south of England. The girl's beauty flowered far beyond either of her sisters', and so did her good sense. She seemed to share exactly her mother's outlook, which was the more insidious for being veiled beneath an appearance of open-mindedness. Belinda, Mrs Gould said, was grown-up now and must make her own decisions. It was just that some decisions would be mad, and inflict a burden of pain on the family which, after all the disasters to date, and considering its growing poverty, could not be borne.

On their first weekend in Yorkshire, David found he had fallen in love with the girl. How could he have supposed her flashy? She was so kind and sensitive. He wanted to be as close to her as at first he had been distant.

He remembered a saying he had heard somewhere, that you should never marry the only good one of a family. Hers had its drawbacks. Mrs Gould was the least subtle of snobs. In company, she would ask him whether he knew such-and-such an Etonian, often someone ten or twenty years older than himself. As for Mr Gould, he had a gentle air, but had abandoned any attempt to keep off gin. On the Saturday evening of that first weekend, he was visited by Barry Pugg, who had a large belly and whose speech David could barely make out. The only reason to warm to his future brother-in-law was that Mrs Gould shuddered at the sight of him.

The Goulds' house was dilapidated. It had been built in a rudimentary gothic manner in the late nineteenth century, by a businessman who wanted a country villa. Mr Gould bought it on settling in Yorkshire, and finding it far too large to heat, knocked the back half of it down. This was the last improvement he attempted: the scale of the work needed to put the rest of the place in order was already so great as to deter him from starting. The stone walls were strong enough, but the roof had half a dozen weak spots.

Mrs Gould clung to the idea that the more dilapidated a house, the more aristocratic its appearance. She developed the preposterous notion that when David and Belinda were married, they would take over the place. One day she amazed him by pointing out the site of the old stables, and suggesting it would be the best place to build new ones.

In these outlandish surroundings Belinda's loveliness was even more conspicuous. To see what he would be taking her from gave him great hope of success. He thought with pleasure of all the things he could give her.

His confidence alarmed her. How could she ever feel so strongly about him? David's devotion was fanatical, and entailed the terrible affliction of retrospective jealousy. The thought of her previous lovers tormented him. She had always regarded herself as quite sparing, considering the number of men who pursued her and the prevailing idea that you could not have too much sex. David, however, hated the idea of these pursuers, let alone that she should have turned and yielded to any of them.

When they had been lovers for some months, she asked him if he could be more romantic, meaning, among other things, more tender. He misunderstood and bought her a present of some French underwear. She liked it, and especially the idea of him buying it, though she had to get the shop to change most of it as it was the wrong size. He attended to her slightest whim, was determined she should be protected. If he went away on exercise, he worried about her.

Before asking her to marry him, he steeled himself to tell her about his parents. She knew he was an only child, his mother living in Argentina and his father dead.

'I haven't told anyone before,' he said.

'You needn't be afraid I'll repeat it.'

'My mother left my father and me when I was five.'

'How awful,' she said, taking his hand.

27

'She went off with one of my father's polo friends.'

'Terrible for you.'

'That wasn't all. I went to be looked after by my god-mother. Then we heard my father had been killed in a shooting accident. For a long time I believed them.'

'It was deliberate?'

He nodded.

'You poor, poor thing.'

'My father was a soldier too. I thought he should have gone and killed the man who took my mother. I thought when I was grown up I'd go and kill him.' Belinda imagined a little boy waving a toy sword towards Argentina. 'Unfortunately he died before I got the chance.'

'Haven't you seen your mother since?'

'She's never been back or expressed any desire to see me. People here took rather a dim view. She did once say I could go and stay in the Argentine with her and her third husband, but I didn't want to. After that she didn't even write.'

Belinda put her arm round him. She could think of nothing to say.

'I think I've got over it now. Especially if . . . '

'What?'

'Nothing.'

He waited a few days before proposing. She asked for more time. She couldn't push him away so quickly. This man who looked impervious to feeling hung on her breast like an infant. Besides, she was fond of him, and was becoming more so; and she thought he would improve. His life in the army was too isolated. She encouraged him to renew old friendships. Jenny Scott-Woodhouse observed, patronizing as usual, that 'David takes being dragged out of his shell so well from you.'

He was from a smarter, more privileged background than Belinda's. When she saw the Life Guards jingling through London in their scarlet and silver uniforms, she felt proud. She had been shown the eighteenth-century stables at Horse

Guards where they kept a dozen or so of their mounts, and had made appreciative remarks to the trooper or NCO or whatever – she could not understand the system of ranks – who was on duty; knowing she reflected credit on David as she did so.

She had also been shown the rooms looking onto White-hall where the Captain of the Queen's Life Guard stayed. There was, she remembered, a framed bedbug over the double bed. David said Horse Guards was the traditional front gate to Buckingham Palace, and that Queen Victoria had once arrived to find the guard drunk; since when an officer had ridden down each day from Hyde Park for the four o'clock inspection. History was alive in the regiment's daily routine. She enjoyed being more intimately connected with it than the tourists outside could hope to be.

She felt proud, too, when David stayed at her parents' house to go hunting. He would come home tired, spattered, bruised and extraordinarily content, feigning ignorance of the grandees with whom he had flung himself about the countryside. 'I met a very nice pawnbroker from Leeds,' he might say. Her mother was, however, able to become loudly indignant on his behalf when he lost a day because, the hunt secretary informed him in advance, guests were barred – owing, as they later discovered, to a visit by the Prince of Wales. Mrs Gould almost turned republican.

David never made anything of the fact that he was rich, but it was clear his wife would want for nothing. They visited Paris: he expected Belinda would buy some dresses. Surely that was what women did in Paris? A couturier sent one of the bills to her. It was shockingly high, but when, with considerable embarrassment, she passed it on to David (she would have paid it herself if it had been within her means) he did not turn a hair.

On the night before he flew to Zimbabwe, he again asked her to marry him.

'Yes,' she said; and the exalted look with which he greeted the reply almost seemed enough.

29

He lamented that he had no time to go and get an engagement ring; said he would send one, which she could have altered if it didn't fit.

'Why don't we keep it a secret until you come back, and then you can get me a ring in London?' she countered.

'All right,' he said slowly, since this was what she wanted.

As soon as he got back, he made for her flat to give her a magnificent diamond ring he had acquired in South Africa.

Three

On the morning after the dinner, Belinda awoke feeling
better than for months past. The party had been a great
success. She stretched herself beneath the duvet, enjoying
the sleepiness of her body and wondering why she seemed
so happy. Her sense of well-being must spring from those
embraces. It was unnatural to go for months without the
touch of another person. He had bruised her lips and scraped
her skin, but these and the lingering taste of him helped to
remind her what had happened.

The beauty of it was that not much had happened. She
had not gone too far. He made his request for sex without
responsibility and she rejected it. She escaped by her own
good judgement, was more in control than ever, because
she felt less tense. As a last fling before getting married, it
was laughably tame.

Her telephone rang. She stopped with her hand over it,
reassuring herself that she would make an excuse if he asked
to see her.

'Hello?'

'I hope I haven't woken you,' Hamish said.

'I was already awake.'

'I just wanted to thank you for the party. I thought you'd
be gone if I left it any later.'

'I've arranged to take the day off.'

'You're sure I didn't wake you?'

'Quite sure.' It was hearing the wrong voice that upset her.

'Well, as I say, we both wanted to thank you for a marvellous evening.'

'I'm glad you and Ann-Louise could come.'

'She enjoyed it every bit as much as I did.'

'Thanks for ringing. See you soon.'

'There was just one other thing.' Long pause. 'I hope, what I mean is I hope we didn't make life awkward for you by leaving when we did. I just thought the way he behaved was abominable, saying he'd come with us and then asking you if he could stay.'

'But I told him he could.'

'Yes, well, it seemed to me it would have been difficult for you to say anything else. I wonder whether he realized how it might appear to other people if he stayed behind with a hostess who was, if I may say, looking' – What was the term he wanted? Man-hungry? – 'radiant.'

'You and I have been to millions of dinner-parties where someone stayed behind with the hostess.'

'Yes, but that was when he was her boyfriend. It's quite different in yours and what's-his-name's case. Ann-Louise and I are both looking forward to, well, you know, to you settling down, and it won't help if you start entertaining penniless young Jewboys at one o'clock in the morning.'

'As a matter of interest, Hamish, are you both anti-Semitic, or is it just you? Is Ann-Louise there?'

'She had to get into work early. Of course we're not anti-Semitic. We're pro-Belinda.'

'Thank you for taking it upon yourself to warn me, Hamish. Since only you and Ann-Louise know I was alone with the Jewboy last night, and I'm sure you won't ruin my reputation by telling anyone else, I can promise you I'm free for you to make a pass at whenever you want.'

'But what about David?' he blurted.

'You'd better ask him first. He should get here tonight.'

She put the phone down and went to do the washing up.

The sofa was still where Tom had pushed it. Afterwards she had a bath, and then she sat for a long time. The phone did not ring again. She wished she hadn't been so content.

Hamish kicked himself. He wasn't anti-Semitic. Some of his best friends were Jews. The days were past when they chose to join the Labour Party because it was less prejudiced. There was, of course, some residual anti-Semitism in England, but it was of the mildest sort and anyone who took it seriously was being paranoid. All the same, he wished the word 'Jewboy' hadn't slipped out – it was foolish, he didn't mean it in a racist way and now he would have to grovel to Belinda to stop it affecting their friendship.

Nor did she think he was trying to make a pass at her. Like him, she picked up the nearest insult to throw, despite the fact it was completely inappropriate. After all, he was engaged to Ann-Louise.

He had simply been keeping his promise to David, to keep a protective eye on Belinda. Her behaviour was incomprehensible. She too was engaged, so it was out of the question that she would have anything to do with Tom, but why then had she let him stay?

There was a second promise Hamish had let himself make, to tell David if someone unsuitable should trouble Belinda. Honouring this was inconceivable, so there was no point thinking about it.

There was no point thinking about Tom, Belinda told herself. She wasn't even going to ring him. She couldn't, however, prevent herself from being angry with Hamish. 'Jewboy' was disgusting. There was envy at the bottom of it; envy that Tom seemed so at ease with himself, and with her as a woman, while insulting the lifestyle of her gentleman yuppie guests by refusing to imitate it.

She was seized by the idea that something of his might

have fallen down the back of the sofa and need returning. Pulling off the cushions, she ran her hand deep into its recesses and found a twopence piece surrounded by fluff.

Suppose she called at his studio in Ealing – she had the address – what would she say? 'I was just on my way to' – she looked at the map of the tube in her diary but there seemed to be nowhere beyond Ealing – 'I was just passing and thought I'd drop in.' Pathetic. To be seen chasing him was unacceptable.

Tom might ring her to say thank you, but she doubted it. Most likely he would do nothing. She had pulled herself together at the end of the evening and sent him away in a final sort of way. What would she do if she were him? She couldn't imagine. She might invite herself to a film, but not today, and today was the last day of her freedom. She looked at her watch. It was noon. There was still time to go to Ealing and have lunch. She dithered. If only David had come on time, she would not have been confronted by this liberty.

Last night she had forgotten to tell her guests that she was looking for a tenant for her second bedroom. She could ring Tom and ask if he knew someone. What if he didn't? What did she say then? She looked at her watch. It was 12.13. It would be a betrayal of David to go and see that lovely boy. She was going to stop thinking about him.

Picking up the telephone, she dialled the first part of the number, put it down again. Her hand left a trace of sweat on the receiver. The right course was to be as straightforward as he had been when the others left last night. She walked round the room, breathing in deeply, like someone plucking up courage to dive into a cold pool. It was too ridiculous. She had wasted an hour. She decided not to ring him. Approaching the telephone obliquely, as if to take it by surprise, she read the number off the open page of her diary and dialled.

At the third ring she decided she would hang up after one more. She took the receiver away from her ear, thought it had been answered, tugged it back, heard a long silence before the ringing again became audible, ran her free hand over her face, felt relieved her initiative had come to nothing. This afternoon she was having her hair done. She started to make a mental list of things she must get while she was out.

As before, a stranger answered the telephone and went to fetch Tom.

'Hello?'

'Hello. It's Belinda.'

'Hello! I was going to phone and thank you for last night. I hope your friend Hamish didn't get the wrong idea about us. It was my fault if he did.'

'Actually, he rang me this morning. You've ruined my reputation.'

'How can I apologize? I'll have to emigrate.'

'I'm afraid you will.'

'Just tell me where.'

'Zimbabwe is fairly remote.'

'Any chance of seeing you before I leave?'

'As it happens there is. I'm not working today. I'd rather like to see your studio.'

'Let's have lunch.' He told her how to find the place, said it would be easy by car from Hammersmith.

There wasn't time to devote proper thought to her appearance. She went as she had dressed after the bath, snatching up a waxed coat and, as an artistic touch, a bright red beret. But the row of about a hundred and ten discreet cosmetics on her bathroom shelf, the gleam of her hair and chic of her brown leather handbag, the sumptuous felt of the beret, her sensational figure clad in a cashmere jersey and jeans, all contributed, Tom thought, to the look of a call girl on a day out from Shepherd Market.

His studio was in a disused factory set back from the road behind a row of houses. A sign on the pavement advertised 'Pottery for sale', with an arrow pointing down a cinder track. Belinda found herself in a yard, from which a door

35

gave entry to a large, empty shed. Other people, including a carpenter, seemed to occupy some of the rooms leading off this. At the far end there were two kilns, a trestle table with pots on it and a door bearing the notice: 'Tom Coleman and William Petrie, potters. Please knock.'

She knocked. Tom opened. He wore jeans which were spattered with paint and through at one knee; a jersey in holes at the elbows.

'Hi.' He kissed her fleetingly. 'I'm a bit mucky,' he said, holding his hands away from her to the sides. 'Come in and I'll clean myself up.'

The studio was very small, an irregular square without windows, lit by a skylight. It had a concrete floor, sloping in the middle to a drain. Work benches, two potters' wheels and an old-fashioned sink were ranged against the walls, to which, at head height, makeshift shelves had been fastened. These carried work in various stages of progress. Tom rinsed his hands under the tap, wiping them on a filthy rag.

'The gas cylinder in the heater's run out. I hope it won't get too cold for you.'

'Are we staying here?' She had expected they would go out.

'Yes. I've bought some food.'

'Let me see what you've done this morning.'

'I started a bit late, thanks to your party. I'm making these moulds for dishes.' He explained the process by which one created a mould. There were technical problems, caused by the intended flatness of the dishes, which he had not yet solved.

'What's this?' she asked, looking at a piece of pottery in different colours with numbers attached.

'I'm mixing glazes,' he said. 'I like the ones where the colours run into each other.'

'And this?'

'A table-lamp. I'm having trouble with that, too.'

She wanted to examine his finished work.

'We've sold most of it. You see, we're still in quite a

36

preliminary stage. After the degree show at college, it took a long time to find this place. There are a few bits and pieces out here.'

He took her back to the trestle table.

'That's a pretty mug.'

'William does those to pay his share of the rent.'

He explained more about the pottery. His partner had over-fired a load of pots and ruined the inside of one kiln. They were waiting for spare parts from Stoke.

She sat on a stool, aware she had not absorbed most of what had been said. It struck her that the pottery could not possibly pay in its present state, but she did not wish to sound commercial. This was the most down-at-heel place she had been to for a long time. It was touching how pleased he was by it.

'If only you were a painter,' she said.

'You mean I could paint you?'

'Your studio might be more comfortable.'

He spread out the food on a piece of newspaper: bread, pâté, cheese, tomatoes, apples. 'I hope that's enough. There was only time to go to the shop round the corner. I've got soup as well.' He heated water in an electric kettle. 'These are special packets without additives,' he said, wiping a mug with the dirty rag.

'Are you into health food?'

'Not at all. It just tastes nicer. Is tea all right to drink?'

'Fine,' she said, looking at the stain on the bread knife.

'It won't come off,' he said.

She cut some slices of bread, sat down again. 'You're too thin,' she observed. 'You can't be eating properly. I should think you weigh less than I do.' She wanted him to come and sit on her lap. Instead he made the soup in two mugs, and a pot of tea, and sat down on another stool.

'This is delicious,' she said, though neither the pâté nor the cheese was good. They came out of the mean little packets you saw in late-night stores. She put her hands round the mug of soup, shivered, wondered if she was going to be sick. He was on his feet again, busy washing two more mugs, doubtless spreading clay over them with that rag. Placing her feet on a high cross-strut of the stool, she wrapped her arms round her knees, resting her forehead on them as though in prayer. With her eyes shut, she wondered why she had come to this clammy little cell. He was deliberately avoiding her. He must have repented of last night.

At the touch of his hand on her shoulder, she remained as still as she could. Her breathing quickened. He felt he was accepted, because not rejected. Very slowly, she turned her head and touched her lips against his hand. It was almost out of reach. She betrayed no haste. He let her have more of it. She could taste the clay which he had failed to wash off. With his free hand, he took off her beret and put it on his head. Her hair fell forward over his hand. He looked down at her. She was kissing him, caressing his fingers with her tongue and lips. He twisted a lock of blonde hair round his spare hand and wondered how far this was going to go.

William Petrie wore training shoes. He made no noise until he kicked the door open and saw his partner in a red beret, one hand buried in a mass of someone's hair, the other holding a tress. The door jammed open against the uneven floor. With difficulty, William kept control of the pile of boxes he was carrying, stepping forward to put them on the bench among the pâté, cheese and bread.

'Spare parts,' he said.

Belinda and Tom disentangled themselves. 'My beret doesn't suit you,' she said, repossessing it.

'William, this is a friend of mine who's visiting,' Tom said.

'Belinda Gould,' she said.

'How do you do,' William replied. 'I can come back later.'

'No, no. I couldn't drive you out of your studio. I've been admiring your mugs. Tell me, how are you going to sell them?'

'You may have seen our sign on the pavement.'

'In quantity, I meant.'

'You're supposed to take photographs and samples round the shops. I'm going to do that as soon as I've time. Just now, I'm trying to placate Tom by mending the kiln.'

'Let me take them round the shops for you.'

'We couldn't put you to the trouble,' Tom said. He had moved the food to one side and was opening a box.

'I work for an interior designer,' Belinda pointed out. 'I could find out which are the most likely shops.'

'There's a lot of work I want to do before I start selling things,' Tom said.

'You have someone to pay the rent,' William observed. 'I think Belinda would be a brilliant saleswoman.'

'Maybe I could help you get started. But if Tom's not worried about money . . . '

'Let's think it over,' William said. 'We haven't got enough stuff to photograph yet. Can I eat some of this?'

'What about you?' Tom said to her.

'I've had plenty, thanks. I can see I'm going to be in the way.'

'I'll walk with you to your car.'

'Take this as a sample,' William said, giving a mug to her. 'Mind how you go,' he added, when his partner was already outside the door.

They went to the car. Tom frowned. She was much too fine to let her fob him off again. He stood by the passenger door waiting for her to let him in. She looked at him across the roof of the car and wondered who paid his rent. A lorry swept past, almost squashing him.

'Hurry up,' he said.

She opened her door, lent across and unlocked his. He got in, looking straight ahead. She had no need to go along with his rudeness.

'I've a hair appointment,' she said.

'Can't you cancel it?'

'I'm not going to. Anyhow, you should get back to work. I only came to have lunch with you.'

'So far you've had my hand.' She could hear the reproach: you led me on. But kissing a man did not necessarily mean you wanted to sleep with him. Some men, as well as women, were quite relieved to stop at kissing.

'I think we'd better stop seeing each other,' she said, 'if you're going to be so demanding.'

'Why don't we meet once more, to see how we get on?' he said. 'Before I go to Zimbabwe.'

'Just once, maybe.'

'Tonight, for example.'

'It's not as easy as you think. I'm getting married.' That was the security she'd spent years moving towards. 'When he's back I can't see you.'

'When's that?'

'His plane should land this afternoon.'

'Since you're engaged to him, there's no harm seeing me.'

'I'll invite David, too,' she said with an unhappy laugh.

He leant over and kissed her. There was no ambiguity in the way she kissed.

Some time later she got out her diary. 'You haven't space for me,' he said, peering over.

'No,' she said, and shut it; smiled that he was taken in; reopened it.

'How about Sunday night?' he said, thinking to joke by suggesting an impossibly distant time.

'Fine,' she said. 'Let's make it Sunday night. I'll have had enough of Gloucestershire by then. If I can't manage it, I'll let you know.'

'You mean you've no evening free before?'

'It is Wednesday. It wouldn't be right to let David down.'

'I can see how reliable you are,' he said, kissing her.

'It's not long.'

'Yes it is.'

'You go and make some beautiful pots. Whoever pays your rent will be sad if you don't do that.' She leant over and kissed him goodbye.

'We kept men have a hard time of it,' he agreed, sitting tight.

'Give me a ring on Friday.'

'This is hopeless,' he said. 'We met each other last night and again today. Why should we wait so long? I'll come round tonight.'

'If David's held up, I might be able to come to you.'

'I was chucked out of my flat. I'm sleeping on William's floor. Expect me at seven.'

'You mustn't,' she protested, but he had slid from the car. He was outrageous. It was fun being outrageous. But what about David? She was so pleased by Tom's eagerness to see her, she tried not to think about David.

Four

Tom got to her flat first. She had thought over the situation during the afternoon and decided it would be wrong to let him in. When he arrived, however, this seemed unduly brusque.

'I told you I'd see you on Sunday,' she said as she led the way up the stairs, irritated by her own softness.

'I told you I'd come tonight.'

'You shouldn't do that to me. It's very inconsiderate.'

'Is this very inconsiderate?' he asked, trying to catch hold of her.

'Yes it is,' she said, evading him. 'How do you think I can relax with David about to turn up?'

'I'll hide under the table.'

'If you did that I'd know not to trust you another time.'

He sat down on the sofa.

'Unless you go away, I won't let you in again.'

He went on sitting there, in an insufferably conceited manner, until she came up behind him and spilt a mug of cold water over his head.

He jumped up with an angry shout and chased her into the kitchen. She screamed with laughter and fear. Holding her against the sink, he tried to fill a cup with water. She stood still for a moment, then jogged his elbow so the water splashed harmlessly across the draining board. They looked at each other, breathing fast, transfixed.

'You're wet!' she said, moving a lock of hair up over his forehead with the tip of her finger.

He bent towards her. She gazed at his eyes and saw his attention fastened on her lips; came forward to kiss him.

The bell rang.

'David!'

'Why answer it?' he said. 'It might be the Jehovah's Witnesses.'

'Let me go.'

He gave way, seeing that this time she could not be stopped. While she rearranged a damp cushion on the sofa and cast an anxious glance over the rest of the room, he crawled under the dining-table.

'In the bedroom!' she said. 'The bedroom cupboard.'

'It's fine here, thanks.'

She adjusted a chair or two. He couldn't be seen unless you peered. If someone sat on the sofa, facing the fireplace, he would have the table behind him.

The bell rang again.

'Damn both of you,' she said, and went to answer it.

David flung his arms about her in such a way that he could not see her face. Her hesitations were no more than he would have expected from one so delicate.

They went upstairs. She put on Elgar's *Pomp and Circumstance Marches* – David was bored by music but had once admitted he liked this; Tom might or might not like it but would get it through a loudspeaker close to his ear – and sat down on a chair.

'How was the bush?' she asked.

'You couldn't turn that down a shade, could you?'

'Of course. Sorry.' She went back to the stereo and reduced the volume.

'What was it you asked?'

'How was the bush?'

'The bush is still very beautiful, but it's not the country it was.'

'Did you arrest lots of ivory poachers?'

'Mostly we shot them. In fact, we trained people. That's what we're there for.'

He was sitting on the sofa. She was some distance away. He felt a desperate need to break the ice and show he wasn't dull.

'Funny chap took over from me,' he said. 'From the Hampshires. We had a week together while I showed him the ropes. Never stopped telling jokes.'

'What like?'

'Oh, I don't know. I'm no good at remembering.'

'Try.'

'Here's one, yes. What did they use in Africa before they had candles?'

'I can't imagine.'

'Electric light!'

She heard a muffled snort from under the dining-room table.

'Not funny,' she said.

'There was another one you won't like.'

'Then don't tell it,' she said, going to sit by him. 'You've never even said hello to me.'

'I'll forget how it goes unless I tell you,' he said, putting an arm round her. 'What's the difference between a terrorist and a woman with pre-menstrual tension?'

'I haven't the faintest idea.'

'At least you can negotiate with a terrorist!'

She burst into noisy laughter. 'I didn't think you'd come back from Africa telling bad-taste jokes,' she said.

'It wasn't my joke, it was the fellow from the Hamp-shires',' he said, encouraged by her enjoyment. 'Utterly common, but an awfully funny fellow.'

'Yes.' She knelt on the sofa and bent down to embrace him. He could not see that over the back of the sofa she was manipulating a dining-chair, in order to jab someone else in the ribs. She saw Tom retreat legs first from his hiding place and crawl towards the corridor; enveloped David the more completely until she heard the downstairs door slam.

Once that had happened she went and took off Elgar.

'I was enjoying it,' David said.

'I wasn't.'

He fingered the small box in his pocket. She came back to the sofa; looked ill at ease.

'It feels strange seeing you again, but I think it often does when one's looked forward to something so much,' he said.

'What were the women like in Zimbabwe?'

'I didn't meet any.'

'You must have done!'

'Nothing to worry about there,' he smiled.

'What shall we do this evening?' she said, hardly returning his embrace.

'I wouldn't mind a drink first.'

'I'm sorry! I feel all nervous!'

'I should have brought a bottle of fizz,' he said. 'I dropped my bag and came straight here.' He needed to see for himself how she was.

'I had Hamish and Matthew and that lot drinking me out of house and home to welcome you back last night.'

'Did you tell them?'

'What?' She was fetching ice.

'About our engagement.'

'No, but I think they knew.'

'I told Jenny before I went away,' he confessed.

'You shouldn't have.'

'Sworn to secrecy.'

'It's nothing to do with Jenny,' she said, giving him his whisky and soda and sitting by him on the sofa. 'Added to which, she's the most frightful gossip. And she patronizes me.'

'Darling, we've waited years,' he said, feeling the box.

'If you love me, you shouldn't mind waiting.'

'Don't be cross,' he asked, trying to sound patient. 'If you love me, you shouldn't want to make me wait for ever.' He took the box out and put it on the small stretch of sofa between them. Though he knew the moment was wrong, he could not stop himself.

'David . . . '

'Belinda?'

'I'm sorry, I'm very fond of you but I don't think I can marry you.'

He turned white.

'Are you marrying someone else?' he asked.

She shook her head; tried to hold him, but he insisted on standing up. Bitterness was rising in him. He must hurry, or it would pour out.

'Thank you for letting me know so quickly,' he said, thinking of the years he had been devoted to her.

'I couldn't do it before! I didn't know.'

'So what changed? What did I do? Did I do too much?'

'You did nothing wrong. It's me, I just know I don't feel as I should. Won't you stay?'

But the only way he could give the impression he was in control of himself was to leave at once.

'I believe you're rather fond of Belinda,' Ann-Louise remarked a few minutes later to Hamish. They were in the sitting-room of his little house off the top of Kensington Church Street. In theory she still lived in Islington, sharing a flat with a girl from university, but in practice she was usually here.

'Yes,' he said. 'I've known her for years.'

'Did you ever have an affair with her?'

'Good heavens, no.' Awkward question, as he had never thought himself a match for Belinda. Buried somewhere in Hamish's attachment to Ann-Louise was the comfortable belief that she was not too good for him. Her plainness did not rebuke his own. She had the figure of a boy. An ideal woman like Belinda would have every reason, and opportunity, to find someone else.

The defect in this calculation was that many men found

Ann-Louise highly attractive. They did not object that she failed to conform to the page-three stereotype. There was sensuality in her bearing, mischief in her eye. Her latest mischief was to engage herself to a man whom nobody would have believed suitable for her.

'So will David stay to supper?' she asked. Hamish's best man had just telephoned, was coming round and would meet Ann-Louise for the first time.

'I don't know. He wants to talk to me. He sounded in a frightful state.'

'So you'd like me out of the way?'

'You must dine with us. I want you to get to know him.'

There was a rap at the front door. She went to the kitchen and Hamish let David in.

'When did you last see Belinda?'

'Yesterday. The dinner to welcome you back.'

'What's happened?'

'I don't know.'

'Well something has. Yesterday she was all eagerness to see me.' A slight exaggeration. She was going to marry him.

'Have you seen her since you got home?'

'Just now. She's changed her mind. I don't want to talk about it. I just need to know if there's someone she didn't tell me about.'

'Not that I know of.'

'You're useless.'

Hamish had been flattered that David wanted to confide in him, until he saw he was merely a source of information.

'If I were you,' he advised, 'I'd wait a bit and talk to her again. Maybe send her some flowers.'

'Well you aren't me,' David said, getting up. At that point Ann-Louise entered; was introduced.

'I'm sorry to interrupt, but I was hoping you'd stay to dinner and I need to know how much food to cook,' she said. Hamish was delighted she sounded so domestic, though he had bought the food himself and it only needed heating.

47

'I think –' David began.

'But if you're expected elsewhere?'

'I'm not expected.'

'We expected you last night.'

'Did anything happen?'

'Nothing,' Hamish said.

'You weren't there,' Ann-Louise observed.

'I won't stay, thank you.' The pair of them were useless.

'I can understand why she's refused him,' Ann-Louise said as soon as David had gone. 'He's so unyielding. Not like you.'

'Darling, you've put your finger on the whole difference between us. You see, I'm a concessionary Conservative, who believes in giving in to changes you can't stop, whereas David's a diehard. What this means –'

'Anyway,' she said, 'at least we've established that your mother can't possibly have them both to stay. So as one of your famous concessions, I think we ought to ask Belinda if she'd like to bring someone else.'

'That's not a concession, darling. She realizes any friend of hers would be welcome at my mother's.'

'Even Tom Coleman?'

'She'd never want to bring him.'

'Then there's no harm asking her.'

'I think, darling, it would be rather rude to Belinda to ask if she wants to bring him.'

A classic tactic, Ann-Louise thought, when you're trying to get your own way: pretend to be doing it for someone else's sake.

'Your friends the Eliots had him to stay in Wales.'

'That was different. He'd met their daughter at art college. She's gone to Australia now.'

'Her maiden heart broken by Tom, I suppose.'

'That's an idea. I'll try to find out.'

'I didn't mean it seriously.'

'Darling, you don't know the type. There are lots of men who just take advantage of women.'

'I can't imagine why you're so determined to guard Belinda.'

It was not the moment to mention his telephone call of that morning.

'Though we ought to thank her for last night,' Ann-Louise went on.

'I rang her this morning.'

'Who answered the phone?' she laughed.

'She did, of course,' Hamish said, taking a moment to catch her drift. Ann-Louise started to kiss him, ruffling his hair and still laughing. He was confused. He adored his little wife, as he already thought of her, but every so often he felt like a man dragged onto the dance floor to perform steps he did not know.

Five

Hamish's mother's house in Gloucestershire had ten bedrooms. She found it cramped, for, as she told visitors, her father-in-law's house in Ireland had three times the number. Her husband, an insurance broker, grew tired of this remark and observed that quantity of bedrooms was not everything, and later, when she persisted in using the measure, that her own parents' house was a third the size of Wolverley Hall, the place he had bought on moving to England. He also humiliated her when she dragged 'Charles Stuart' (meaning King Charles I or II) into the conversation, by adding 'No relation'. What was the point of being called Stuart and throwing it away?

Apart from minor arguments of this sort, they had lived contentedly until he was killed in a car accident. Their only son was then fourteen years old and at Marlborough. She had objected that it was a middle-class school, but Mr Stuart pointed out that her brother's children had done well there. He said nothing would induce him to send his son to Wellington, where he himself, intended for the army, had been.

In death, Mr Stuart underwent an apotheosis. He would have admitted, if necessary, that his family had for a short period done well in linen, but his widow presented him as a scion of the most ancient nobility. She was a generous woman who could imagine nothing better for him.

Mrs Stuart always said her son could bring friends home. She was good like that, and so was he. Nothing had to be said about who would suit. David Cheney was a favourite, and so was Belinda. The girl proved that the allure of a film star could be combined with good behaviour: that the devil did not have all the best looks. Ann-Louise was harder to fathom. Mrs Stuart could find no clear fault with her (and was already working hard to bring a peer remotely connected to her future daughter-in-law into the immediate family circle), but she doubted they would ever be as close as, say, she and Belinda already were.

This weekend, Mrs Stuart went to bed quite early on the Friday night, before everyone had arrived. She would see them at breakfast the next morning.

Belinda was first down.

'My dear!' exclaimed Mrs Stuart. 'You usually sleep later than anyone! You're looking uncommon well.' She liked using 'uncommon' in that way. 'Help yourself to breakfast. I hope Hamish told you if there was a friend you wanted to bring, he would be welcome.' She could be intimate with Belinda. She was like a daughter. 'Just as you used to come with David, before we got to know you. He would always bring you.'

'Sometimes,' Belinda corrected. She hadn't accepted all the invitations.

'I'll never forget meeting him at Sandown,' Mrs Stuart said, and told an anecdote Belinda had heard several times before.

'We've decided to stop seeing each other.'

'You're a silly girl when he came all the way from Africa to see you.' Even Belinda needed advice. Mrs Stuart had married when she was twenty-two. Modern girls lingered forever. 'You do like him, don't you?'

'As a friend.'

'He adores you,' Mrs Stuart replied, disappointed by 'as a friend'.

Hamish was next to arrive.

'Have you heard?' he asked, helping himself to a large plateful of kedgeree from the sideboard. 'It was on the radio. Cedric Williams has had a heart attack.'

'Really, my dear Hamish, I have no idea who Cedric Williams is,' Mrs Stuart said. 'Do you have any idea, Belinda?'

'None whatever,' she said. Hamish had rung the day after his 'Jewboy' taunt, apologized at length and urged her still to come for the weekend ('We haven't asked David'), but she looked on him with a colder eye.

'He's member for one of the Essex seats on the Thames estuary,' Hamish explained. 'It used to be Labour but it's safe Tory now. As it happens, I know him a bit. He asked me to speak at his association dinner.'

'A heart attack,' his mother said. 'It's too awful. Provided he dies, what chance do you have of getting the nomination?'

'I should think that even if he pulls through, the doctors will tell him to retire. He's so fat. It's an interesting constituency, though not, on the face of it, one where I would be expected to do well. Full of people who moved out of the East End of London to get away from the blacks, and tell you so. The local association is fanatically in favour of capital punishment and compulsory repatriation.'

'Not for the same people, I suppose!' his mother said. 'Not much point repatriating corpses!'

'Cedric says they're also very keen on corporal punishment,' Hamish continued. 'I expect they'd like to thrash the blacks, or the Hong Kong Chinese, or whoever it was, before they put them onto the ships. The thing which really infuriated them about Cedric was that the year he came top of the ballot, he wouldn't introduce a bill for the castration of rapists. A missed opportunity, they thought.'

'It's horrible,' Belinda agreed. 'I drove through once with a friend who took me to see his greyhound. Nothing but oil refineries and ribbon development. Those ghastly 1930s houses you used to see on bypasses, with bogus Tudor gables and expensive new plate-glass windows knocked into

52

them, and plastic stonework stuck over pebbledash. Neo-Georgian front doors.'

'I'd forgotten you were such an architectural critic,' Hamish said.

'I do work for an interior designer.'

'Well, no doubt you and your employer look down your noses at those suburban houses, but they're what people want. They've gone up in the world, got out of the slums, so why shouldn't they feel proud of the fact? Anyway, that's what I told them in my speech. Give the people what they want. I agree their houses are ghastly. If you ring the two-tone doorbell and are unlucky enough to be asked in, you find the interiors are frightful too.'

'You're such a hypocrite, Hamish,' Belinda said. 'If their views on race are disgusting, and their houses are ghastly, you should have said: "Don't give the people what they want."'

'Considering I was a last-minute stand-in, I thought I did rather well. It was a pragmatic speech.'

'You sound as though you want to have a go at getting it,' Mrs Stuart said. 'But I'm sure a traditional Tory like you wouldn't stand a chance. They'd rather have a second-hand car salesman. Added to which, it would be unfair on Ann-Louise. Good morning, my dear.'

Her prospective daughter-in-law had entered with several other guests.

'What wouldn't be fair?' she asked, pouring herself a cup of coffee.

'Taking the Essex seat which Hamish is so excited about,' her prospective mother-in-law said.

'I don't want to hold him back.'

'Well,' Hamish announced, 'if Cedric is alive next week, I'll go and see him.'

'How noble,' Belinda said.

'It is actually rather noble of me. If you want that seat, don't let people know you're a friend of Cedric Williams,

53

the man who said we should band together to build a multicultural Britain.'

The whole party had been invited to drinks before lunch in the next village, where a commodity broker and his wife spent the weekends in a converted cowshed. Most people opted to walk there. A few made the mistake of getting ready at once and waited nearly an hour for everyone else to assemble.

Belinda and Ann-Louise walked together, at the back of the party as it straggled off down a field to the stream that marked the edge of the Stuart property.

'Don't we look uniform,' Belinda said. The weekend gear of the townspeople was not very varied. They all wore Barbours.

'Mrs Stuart wanted me to stay and talk about the wedding arrangements,' Ann-Louise confessed. 'I pleaded to be let off until after lunch.' The wedding was to take place in Gloucestershire because her own parents were in the Foreign Office, posted to the Middle East.

'An awful business, a wedding,' Belinda agreed. 'Though I admit I might enjoy arranging my own.' She knew she was being offered an anti-Mrs-Stuart conversation; felt torn between the habit of loyal reticence and a new desire to rebel. She wouldn't mind an anti-this-whole-weekend conversation, including these pointless drinks they were going to. Had she not been telephoned by Mrs Stuart as well as by Hamish, and promised to come, she would have cried off.

'I told Hamish he should ask you if you wanted to bring a friend this weekend,' Ann-Louise said.

'You sound just like Hamish's mother, still trying to pair me off with David.'

'I was wondering whether you wanted to bring Tom.'

Belinda was getting over a stile, before the footbridge over the stream. The others were fifty yards ahead.

'I shouldn't have likened you to Mrs Stuart. She would never have made that suggestion.'

'He stayed with the Eliots, so he must be all right,' Ann-Louise said, imitating Mrs Stuart.

'But do we really know what his background is?' Belinda continued in the same voice.

'Well, as a matter of fact we do,' Ann-Louise said. 'He went to a state school but his father's a builder who made good. They moved out of the East End of London to Essex.'

Belinda's pleasure that they were talking about Tom overcame her doubts about Ann-Louise. Only a residual feeling of caution made her try to maintain a light tone.

'How much did the private detective cost?' she asked.

'The price of a telephone call by Hamish to Mrs Eliot.'

'Economical!'

'But I'm sure you know all this.'

'I'd like to hear Mrs Eliot's account.'

'She said it was a nightmare. He beat Corinna up.'

'Never trust a mother about her children.'

'Hasn't he beaten you up?'

'Who says he's done anything to me?'

'If you don't want him, let's swap.'

'But you're committed to Hamish!'

'Just teasing. I do, however, think that when you're married, it's vital for each partner to keep his or her own friends of the opposite sex.'

'Hamish won't think so. If I were Hamish, I'd be hurt by that. It's not fair on him and it's not fair on the friends. They'd always be wanting more than you had any right to give.'

'It is difficult,' she said gravely. 'I've talked to Hamish. He only half understands it.' Because it's nonsense, Belinda thought.

'That's why we ought to swap,' Ann-Louise repeated. 'Anyone can see you have more in common with Hamish than I do. As for Tom, apart from being delectable, I think I could manage him.'

This was painful. First it supposed that Tom was hers to swap. He wasn't yet. They had not spoken since he hid under the dining-table. She was not certain he would come tomorrow night: he might think she was soldiering on with David. She wondered if it had been rather mean to play the *Pomp and Circumstance Marches* in his ear.

Having flattered her by recognizing her possession of Tom, Ann-Louise insulted her, by suggesting she was unable to manage him.

'The thing is not to take him seriously, even if he does have gorgeous eyelashes,' the girl went on, identifying one of Tom's most enchanting features. 'If you take him seriously, you're finished, and in my opinion it won't even be his fault, any more than it's your fault that David Cheney is mad about you. The problem with David is you've never treated him badly enough, so that he had to give you up. You've been weak. All your sweetness to him has made him more in love.' This stab owed something to an earlier cross-examination of Hamish, but more to her intuition about Belinda.

'How do you know I was sweet to him? I refused him.'

'That must be why everyone thought you were engaged to him.'

'You are nasty.'

'If I were you I'd have a new lover every week. I'd be like Barbara Skelton, though I wouldn't let King Farouk whip me with a dressing-gown cord.'

'I don't know who Barbara Skelton is, but maybe she has a different personality to me. You obviously do.'

'She said she'd have preferred a split cane. The trouble with you is you're too inhibited to admit you're inhibited. It's hopeless. Just as I grow up, inhibitions are coming back. Hamish is so sweet. He has an inhibition about failing to give me orgasms. I suppose that's an inhibition of the people who thought they were getting rid of inhibitions, so it doesn't prove my point, but it took me weeks to shut him up.'

56

'You shouldn't talk about him like that.'

'You're being sweet again.'

'It must be awful to feel obliged to perform, if you're afraid you're going to fail.'

'He hardly ever fails. Maybe I do. All the same, I adore Hamish. If you realized how noble and good he is, you'd reconsider.'

'Boo!' cried the prospective MP, jumping out from behind a tree. 'What would she reconsider? You're not meant to overhear conversations about yourself, but it hasn't done me any damage. You'd have gone the wrong way if I didn't wait.' He took Ann-Louise's arm and lumbered off down a track.

Belinda thought of Tom. Her imagination rushed forward. They might set up a pottery in the country. She wondered where he was now; whether he was alone.

Six

That afternoon, Mrs Stuart took Ann-Louise to talk about
the wedding. Some of the guests played tennis, a couple
went to an antique shop, others visited a house that one of
them wanted to see. Belinda had a sleep on the sofa in the
library, a room which contained very few books; wondered
whether to go back to London to see Tom.

If she could be sure where he was, she would go at once.
She was possessed by the thought that her character was
going to change; that she could stop being cautious and
seize her pleasures.

She had a headache. This visit to Wolverley was going,
she wrongly estimated, to be like all the others. Mrs Stuart
would make intrusive remarks, Hamish would stride ineffec-
tually about, a landed proprietor without land, and tonight
they would dress for dinner – it was one of Mrs Stuart's
foibles to prefer her guests to wear black tie for dinner –
and try to look leisured.

Belinda went to the kitchen in search of a cup of tea and
found the housekeeper, Mrs Millett. Mrs M. put the kettle
on and told her what her alcoholic husband had been doing
since their last talk. It wasn't the violence she minded, but
he spent all their money. And what about Belinda?

'I may be going to start an affair with a younger man,
Mrs M.' She found it easier to confide in people outside her
social circle.

Mrs M. was enthusiastic; wanted details. Belinda supplied them, until Mrs Stuart came to check on the dinner.

'Really, Belinda, hiding away down here.'

'I was having a chat with Mrs M.'

'Don't you agree, Mrs M., that it's time Belinda was married?'

'What's the rush?' Mrs M. replied.

'We shall have to see what we can do. Never say die, Belinda.'

'Thank you, but don't you think I can decide for myself?'

'Yes, my dear, but it's a question of who you're deciding among. Your friends aren't interfering if they introduce you to eligible bachelors.'

'It is a truth universally acknowledged, that a single woman who is thirty-four years old must be desperately in want of a husband.'

'No, Belinda, it is not universally acknowledged, but it is true. It would be all very well to let your hair down and go out on the razzle if you were younger, but at thirty-four you must stop thinking of fun. You've always, thank heavens, been steady, so you surely agree the time has come to make up your mind. Remember that friends who are not so closely involved can usually see things clearer than you can.'

'And you only want the best for me.'

'Precisely.'

Well go to hell, Belinda thought. 'I think I'll go and have a bath,' she said. 'Goodbye, Mrs M. I did enjoy our talk.'

Bathrooms would be in short supply nearer to dinner, when the tennis players and sightseers came in. The best bath at Wolverley was Mrs Stuart's, which Belinda had long been allowed to use. It was twice the size of modern baths and stood in the middle of a former dressing-room.

She was lying motionless in the water when she heard Hamish's voice. There was a clear half-inch separating the bottom of the bathroom door from polished wood.

'Where are you off to now?' he said.

'To see if your mother's bathroom is free,' Ann-Louise

59

replied. 'If you can't see it's an outrageous way for her to behave, you can't see anything.' She rattled the doorknob. 'Fuck. Someone's got here first. I really can't think how you allowed your mother to do it.'

'But I've only just heard,' Hamish said as they faded from earshot.

Tomorrow night, she would be away from the argument, whatever it was, between those three; away from a houseful of people pretending to be friends of Edward VII.

She climbed from the bath, dried herself, put on her dressing-gown and went along the landing to her own room. If she had known where Ann-Louise was sleeping, she would have called on her, to say the bath was free and perhaps to commiserate with the wretched girl about the argument. She was sorry for her. An engagement should be happy.

There were oceans of time. Belinda dressed very slowly. She had a dark red satin dress with some black in it. It was old, but fitted her perfectly; had not been worn for so long that she hoped it had regained a degree of novelty. She was first down. Taking a seat by the fire which had been lit in the drawing-room, she wondered whether she was going to be cold.

Hamish appeared next. Belinda had not read a word of the magazine on her lap. She felt nervous. Perhaps it was the chill of the room: she should get a cardigan.

He looked less at ease than she was. His wing collar bit into his neck and he had reopened an old cut with his razor.

'I must get some more glasses,' he said. 'I wanted, Belinda, to tell you before anyone comes.'

'What about, Hamish?'

'I thought of putting a note under your bedroom door, but that seemed excessive.'

'Simpler to knock.'

'I'm afraid you're not going to be pleased.'

Belinda saw the magazine was open at an article about azaleas. Two more men in dinner-jackets entered.

'Come and get the glasses with me,' Hamish urged her.

'I'm going to run upstairs and find a cardigan,' she said. 'Otherwise I shall freeze.'

'She's stunning,' one of the men said when she had gone.

'Lovely,' Hamish agreed. 'I must find out what's become of the glasses. Help yourselves if those tumblers are any use to you.'

'Is she married?' the man asked, mixing himself a Bloody Mary.

'Single,' his companion said, doing likewise.

'Not even engaged?'

'All yours, as far as I'm aware.'

'Any idea what age she is?'

'Early thirties.'

'Just right. I think when one settles down one doesn't want some flighty young thing. One wants someone who's prepared to settle down, too. Someone who'll look after one.'

'I don't know what makes you think women in their early thirties want to look after you. Most of the women I know seem to be getting divorced. Some of them have children in tow.'

'This one's avoided all that, hasn't she?'

'Come through unscathed.'

'I think I'll offer her a lift back to London.'

'She came in her own car.'

'You're such a defeatist.'

Another man appeared in the doorway. He was tanned and held himself very straight. By the correctness of his evening dress, he demonstrated how scruffy the others were.

'Good evening,' he said, holding out a hand. 'David Cheney.'

'Piers Plumtree,' Belinda's new admirer replied. 'And this is Simon Warde-Smith.'

'How do you do. I believe we've met,' David said to Simon, taking up a position with his back to the fire.

'Come far?' Piers asked.

'Tonight only fifty miles.'

'We were just discussing an absolute peach of a girl,' Piers said. 'What's her name again?'

'Belinda Gould,' Simon answered.

'Yes, Belinda. Quite magnificent, I assure you. She was here a moment ago.'

David had gone to the door, where he met Hamish bearing a tray of glasses.

'I asked whether there would be anyone I knew,' he said, in a voice too quiet for the others to hear. 'I was told "nobody much". In my opinion, Belinda doesn't count as nobody much.'

'There's been the most ghastly cock-up,' Hamish said.

'By whom?'

'Not Belinda. She doesn't know you're here.'

David brushed past him and made for the front door. It was on the far side of the hall, round which, on pillars, ran the first-floor landing. He reached an inner door with a large pane of glass in it, leading into a porch full of boots, sticks, hats, equipment for half a dozen sports. As he put his hand on the doorknob, he glanced back.

Though a chandelier in the middle of the hall obscured his view, he knew from the tilt of her head it was Belinda on the first-floor landing opposite. He hesitated, decided that from her position leaning on the balustrade she must have seen him, felt he could not slink away without showing his face, stepped forward.

They stared at each other. 'Don't worry,' he said. 'I'm leaving.'

She shrugged. His rage at being brought here under false pretences gave way to agony. He turned to hide himself and pulled at the door.

'Welcome to Wolverley!' Mrs Stuart always had shown more enthusiasm for his company than he could feel for hers. She clattered across the hall to embrace him.

'Good evening, Mrs Stuart. I'm just going.'

'But why, David?'

'Because I don't wish to be sprung on someone who thinks, in her infinite wisdom, that it would be better if we did not meet.'

'But I didn't ask you because I wanted to see you! I asked you for her!'

'Did you ask her if she wanted to see me?'

'We talked about you all through breakfast.'

'You asked her, I suppose?'

'Yes, I did. Of course I did. Why shouldn't I ask her?'

'Then I'm afraid there's been a misunderstanding.' He took a step towards the door, grasped the handle for the third time, from weakness looked up again at Belinda. To his surprise, she had not fled. He yearned for her to speak to him. Since their last, catastrophic meeting he had waited for her to show that he need not hide his love, need not fear to hurt her if he expressed it.

When they had been together, she was often reticent, but at least he had been able to declare his feelings for her, and hope that in time she would reciprocate. She never did. After years of uncertainty – of 'fondness', 'wanting to be close to him', loving him while doubting – she let herself be persuaded into a secret engagement; which collapsed as soon as they met again. The only gift he could give her now was his absence, by an effort of self-denial that lacerated his heart.

Mrs Stuart followed David's look back over her own shoulder and saw they were being watched. 'My dear Belinda!' she appealed.

David reminded Belinda of some pathetically faithful guard dog, always trying to do the right thing, never rewarded by his master's affection. If she were kind, he could not help being encouraged. If she were cruel, she would make him suffer, and since it was not her fault she felt nothing for him her sympathy would change to vexation.

'Please tell David not to be so absurd,' Mrs Stuart said. 'He's come all the way here and now he wants to go off without his dinner.'

63

'Oh well, if you've come all this way, you could dine,' she said.

'See! She wants you to stay!' Mrs Stuart said. 'I've a house full of people. I don't think I can be expected to remember what I said to every one of them.'

David knew Belinda did not want him to remain, but had been given just enough excuse to ignore the fact. By the time she came downstairs, he was on the far side of the drawing-room, hidden by a screen of people, and was saying that yes, as chance would have it he had come across Piers Plumtree's cousin called Brown in the Hampshires, had a week with him in Zimbabwe, an awfully amusing fellow. Belinda thought David would come and speak to her, he hoped she would do the same to him, so they did not meet.

They sat down sixteen to dinner. The placement had been done by Mrs Stuart before the scene in the hall. She gave it to Hamish, asking him to tell people where to go. He saw that David had been put next to Belinda and swapped him with Piers.

The meal went off without a hitch. Mrs Stuart's table was long and thin, which meant that David, working hard to develop a conversation about horses, could not see Belinda at the other end. Her distress at wearing a dress she had chosen, but he had paid for, diminished.

By the time Mrs Stuart took the ladies off to the drawing-room, Belinda felt quite relaxed.

David listened tolerantly to Hamish's exposition of the Conservative approach to Europe, pushing the decanter of port past without refilling his glass. At the other end of the table, the talk was livelier. Plumtree was being mocked for his failure to persuade Belinda to go to the cinema with him. When he and his attackers started shouting at each other, Hamish was obliged to stop, though he had reached a vital point about the European Monetary System.

'If you'll only keep quiet for a moment or two, I can explain,' Plumtree managed to say.

'Let him make his excuses,' Simon Warde-Smith put in.

'There's someone else,' Plumtree said, in the moment of silence allowed him.

His friends asked what else he had expected, said he was mad to have thought he stood a chance, inquired who his rival was.

'She says he's nobody I know,' he answered. 'Hamish, do you know who her boyfriend is?'

'No doubt she made him up in order to keep you off,' Hamish said.

'Oh no she didn't,' Plumtree asserted.

'She was spinning you a yarn,' Hamish persisted. 'You don't realize how unattractive you look.'

'She said she preferred younger men,' Plumtree offered.

'That was to make you feel jealous,' someone told him.

'Shut up, Plumbridge,' David said in a ferocious voice.

'The name's Plumtree.'

David hit the table hard with the flat of his hand. 'I don't give a damn what you're called but stop talking about her.'

The tinkle of glass and silver died away. Plumtree decided he would rather snigger to his friends about the loony militarist than insist on his right to talk about Belinda. A sheepish conversation picked up from his end of the table. When it was safe, one of his friends said he doubted whether the army would need the cavalry much longer. Someone else told them David's brother officers thought he was cracked.

'I can't think why I invited Plumtree,' Hamish said to David. 'He seemed all right before.'

'Do you really believe Belinda was just spinning him a yarn?'

'Oh, absolutely.'

'I wouldn't mind if she got married to someone decent.' He meant he would mind terribly but try to put up with it. 'You have promised, though, to tell me if some bastard gets hold of her?'

Hamish nodded. 'Now we're able to have a quiet word, I ought to say how sorry I am you were asked here.'

'But maybe your mother was right. It's no good avoiding

people just because you're fond of them. As a woman she understood that.'

What did David know about women, Hamish wondered. The army had preserved a kind of innocence in him. It was a monastery in which he thought strange, childlike thoughts.

'I think I'm lucky to have met Ann-Louise,' Hamish said, 'because she isn't the same as me. Otherwise I might have become stodgy.' One confidence deserved another. All the same, it was not English. David had got odder, or less able to control himself.

'If you don't mind, I think I'll go,' David said when they were about to join the ladies. He did not want to see Belinda among a crowd of people, where the chances of a proper talk were nil. Other arrangements must be made. 'Please thank your mother for me and say I didn't want to break up the party. And give Belinda my love.'

Seven

Belinda got back to London in good time on Sunday and found a message on her answering machine. Tom would not be able to visit her until late that night.

When he did arrive, he had a suitcase with him.

'What's that?' she asked.

'A suitcase.'

'Did you think you could stay here?'

'I couldn't leave it in the street, could I?'

He looked even more handsome. His self-confidence annoyed her.

'I'm getting a lodger for the spare room,' she said.

'Good idea.'

'The rent's seventy pounds a week, plus a share of bills.'

'Have you any Danish blood?' he asked, sitting down. 'You look Danish to me. Not that I've been there.'

'You behave as if you've got Vandal blood.'

'Perhaps you can civilize me.'

'Do you renounce rape and pillage?' she asked.

'I do.'

'And smashing up telephone boxes?'

'If you insist.'

'In that case you can stay on trial. Your room's opposite the bathroom.'

'What about my conditions?'

'Your conditions?'

67

'It's a bit one-sided. I'd like you to promise me I won't have to hide under the table.'

'David's gone.'

'Or get hit with a chair.'

'Only when you deserve it.'

'And that if you find a lodger, I can move in with you.'

'I won't commit myself to that,' she said. 'The lodger might be nice. Good night.'

After she had retired, he poured himself a glass of whisky and decided it looked a good place to stay.

David left Wolverley Hall in a more cheerful frame of mind. He had thought of a role that would enable him to go on seeing Belinda. By forming a relaxed friendship with her, he would protect her against unwelcome advances. He had been heartened by the way she drove off Plumtree, but others might be harder to repulse. She looked perilously attractive.

He would see her in August, when he was to be best man at Hamish's wedding, but that was months away. The first task was to keep in touch, without making her think he was in pursuit. The telephone was too chancy. You never knew whether you would catch someone at a bad moment. A letter, on the other hand, would look premeditated, and she had never been good at writing back. He hit on it: her place of work, a gallery called Conrad Smith of Knightsbridge, specializing in interior design.

The best thing would be to call one afternoon, when his duties were over but before the gallery closed. There might be the chance of a drink with her; dinner even, if by some fluke she was free. On Monday evening he walked down from Hyde Park Barracks – a barbaric modern edifice, in his opinion, with a grotesque tower – to check the shop's opening hours.

As soon as Tom moved in, Belinda sought a word with her employer. Conrad Smith's visits to the premises named after himself were intermittent, for he was often away visiting clients and suppliers. She caught him on Tuesday.

'Great,' he said, taking her through to his tiny office at the back. There was barely room for the two of them to sit down. 'I've been wanting to talk things through with you.'

He was a South African who had arrived in London a decade ago, and tried to lend tone to his business by employing classy English girls. Belinda detested him. She would never have agreed to be his 'personal assistant' were it not for the short-lived delusion, born of suicidal boredom with her previous job, that Conrad Smith offered a way into the 'creative' world. He had chunky gold buckles on his shoes and chunky gold rings on his fingers, while his trim blazer, made in too light a shade of blue, had chunky gold buttons, but the most odious thing he wore was his hairpiece. He purveyed 'style' to third-rate banks.

As they sat in the tiny room, his knees almost touched hers.

'Now tell me, I'm concerned,' Conrad said, staring at black stockings that vanished into a black leather skirt. Her legs were superb. 'Ever since you came here four months ago you've been highly efficient, but recently you don't seem to have the concentration. You've taken a day or two off, which you never did before, and strictly between ourselves, Sue isn't capable of dealing with clients.' Sue was the accounts girl. 'Now I'm not criticizing. I don't want to pry into your private life. But if you have some problem there, and need a couple of weeks away, just let me know. I won't ask questions. I'd just like to be able to help.'

This show of generosity was so at odds with her knowledge of Conrad, who was sycophantic to people more powerful than himself and bullied everyone else, that Belinda did not know how to reply. She had been ready to answer the charge that several orders had been lost by her slackness.

'It has been a difficult time,' she answered, 'and I'm grateful to you for offering me a holiday. But I think I'd rather soldier on and go away when we shut for August. I've been meaning to apologize that we may have lost one or two orders because I was out. I'll try to make sure it doesn't happen again. To be honest, the real trouble is that I don't find the work very challenging. For example, I've discovered a brilliant potter, but I don't suppose it's even worth mentioning his work to you.'

'Belinda, I can't tell you how glad I am that you decided to open your heart about this to me.' She knew now who he reminded her of. A smarmy, evangelical clergyman. It was horrid being in the same room as him. As for the idea that he would find more interesting work for her to do, it was laughable. In small businesses like his, only the proprietor had interesting work. The rest of the staff were sweated labour. She must, she told herself for the hundredth time, find another job; meanwhile get out of this room. She stood up.

Conrad stood up too. He put his arm round her shoulder. She tried not to shudder.

'Don't run away, and don't ever mention those orders to me again. You just come and tell me if you're ever in trouble,' he said in that clipped way of his, holding her shoulder against him. 'You and I are a great team.'

'Thank you,' she said, trying to break away.

'As for the other point you raised, about challenging work, we ought to discuss that out of the office environment. Are you free for dinner one night this week?'

'I'm sorry, I don't think I am,' she said, sitting down again to evade his hold. With him on his feet, the door was blocked.

'How about next week?' he said, sitting down. 'There must be one night you can manage.'

'I've always wanted to meet Mrs Smith,' Belinda said.

'Mrs Smith is in Durban. Her mother's sick.'

'In that case I couldn't possibly.'

'You don't understand. There would be nothing Mrs Smith could object to. It would be a working dinner between colleagues. You see, Belinda, you're an integral part of the future of Conrad Smith, and at present we're just not using your full potential. You ought to be going on client visits. The sky's the limit for you. You'll have them tied up in knots, especially if you wear that skirt for them.' He leant forward and felt the hem of it. 'That's a great piece of leather, Belinda. You've got natural good taste.'

'I don't think my boyfriend would like me to have dinner with you,' she said, standing up. Conrad jumped up too, resuming his grip on her shoulder. He behaved as if he had established a right to hold her. She wriggled, trying to shake him off, but Conrad found this indescribably arousing. Her breast had brushed against him. One button on her shirt seemed to be crucial.

'Let me tell you about boyfriends,' he said.

'Take your hand off me.'

'Yes. Of course. Let's have some coffee.' He opened the door. 'Sue, could you fix us a couple of coffees?' he called. 'Now sit down. That's right. I don't know the first thing about your boyfriend, but I wonder whether he realizes how far you can go? He's probably so successful himself he doesn't realize you could be a success too. Men are like that. They underestimate women. You've no idea the money you could make if you came into partnership with me.'

'You're wrong about my boyfriend. He's not successful yet. He's a potter.' In reality he was just a non-paying lodger. Last night she'd avoided him by going to a party.

'Let's have him to dinner too!' Conrad could not give up the idea of dinner. 'What sort of stuff does he make?'

'He's designing a new table-lamp.'

'Terrific. When can you show me samples?'

'I'll ask. He doesn't want to be hurried.'

'You ask him, but remember' – he ventured an avuncular pat on her thigh – 'don't ever let a man hold you back.'

She stood up. He sprang upright himself. 'I must go and

71

see Sue,' she said, and turned her head away, waiting for him to open the door.

'Belinda,' he said. 'I've never been much good at expressing myself. I still don't think you see all the advantages of co-operating with me. Let's go to my flat and I can explain.'

She wished she need never say another word to him. 'Open the door,' she said.

'Belinda.' His hand held her arm just above the elbow.

'Let go,' she screamed, surprised by a sudden tightening of his grip.

'Listen to me.'

'Stop it, you creep.'

'Don't you see I'm no threat to you?' He was pushing himself at her, groping at her front. Her bottom hit the edge of his desk. She leant back to give herself room, saw the hairpiece straining after her, hit him across the face with her free hand. He swayed sideways, tripped on her feet and fell. She pulled open the door, hitting him hard in the chest, stepped over the body and ran.

Belinda's protector called at the gallery that afternoon. He wore a navy blue suit and a bowler hat. There was nobody in the showroom: it contained a quantity of fabrics, light-shades and catalogues. He felt intensely nervous about seeing her.

A mousy young woman appeared from the back of the shop.

'Good afternoon,' David said. 'Is it possible to speak to Belinda Gould, please?'

'She's gone home early.'

'Oh dear. Not ill, I hope?' The girl looked doubtful. 'I'm an old friend of hers. Do tell me if anything's the matter.'

'She just grabbed her bag and run out the shop.'

'Didn't she say something?'

'She looked that upset, I don't think she seen me.'

'But why do you suppose she was upset?' David asked,

in the style of a judge coaxing vital evidence from a child witness.

'She's gone into the office for a chat with Conrad.'

'Yes.'

'After a bit he called out to bring them coffee. I'm just boiling up – we've got a place out there to boil up – when I hear Belinda screaming.'

'And what do you think she said?'

'She shouted, "Creep!" Then the door opened and out she run, like I said. A minute later, Conrad come out holding his eye and his side. "Has she gone?" he says. "Yes," I says, "she run out just grabbing her bag. Where would you like your coffee?" He's sat down on that chair. "She could have blinded me," he said, "and I think she's cracked one of my ribs." "Goodness," I said, "whatever possessed her to do a thing like that?" – though I had a pretty good idea, mind. Conrad couldn't take his eyes off her, always sizing her up. I found him sniffing her coat once, dirty old man. Now his wife's in Africa, he thinks he sees his chance.'

'Where is Conrad?'

'He said he was off to see a doctor, but he's been gone hours.'

'Thank you. You've been extremely helpful. I think I need to have a word with him. If I may, I'll wait till you close. It's only fifteen minutes, isn't it?'

'Don't tell him I told you.'

'Certainly not. Just give me a nod if he comes in.'

Conrad returned on the stroke of 5.30. He had a black eye and walked as though in pain. As he stepped through the door, Sue nodded.

'Hello, Conrad,' she said. 'I'm just off.'

'Good afternoon, Mr Smith,' David said when Sue had gone. 'I'm a friend of Belinda Gould's.'

The little man swallowed. 'Pleased to meet you,' he said.

'She was telling me about your pots.'

'Oh yes. What did she tell you about them?' The judge's tone had hardened.

73

'She said they were still at an experimental stage, but you're making a table-lamp. I want straight away to say that I'd like very much to see a sample and shall almost certainly be placing a large order.'

'Thank you. What else do you know about me?'

'Well, that you're her boyfriend. I thought you'd come round. All I can say is I'm sorry about what happened this morning. It was a terrible mistake.'

'What did happen this morning?'

'Well, Belinda asked if she could come to my office for a chat, and I asked Sue to make some coffee for us. Belinda is like a daughter to me, has been ever since she came here. I feel very protective towards her – which naturally you do to a much greater extent – and just lately she's been late back after lunch once or twice, not that I mind, so I wanted to say to her, look, I'm the last person to pry into your private life, but if you need some time off just tell me. Then I asked her to become a partner in the business, and that was when she got upset, because I put a hand on her arm, just to reassure her.' David waited, as though this account did not tally with Belinda's. 'And one of her buttons was coming undone,' Conrad added in desperation, 'and I tried to do it up.'

'Where was this button coming undone?'

'On her shirt.'

'So you had one hand on her arm and one on her breast. I suppose that's how you generally treat your staff?' He wished he had brought a horsewhip with him from the barracks. How could one deal with a man too disgusting to touch? He recalled then that Smith had touched Belinda, and lost control. Picking him up by the lapels of his blazer, David shook him. Then he put him down and held him with one hand, belabouring him with the other. Then he threw him on the floor, picked him up and resumed hitting him. 'Tell me you won't do that again, Smith. Not to Belinda and not to anyone else.'

Dazed by the blows and out of his mind with fear, Conrad

74

failed to react. He was again thrown on the floor and picked up, his nose and lip bleeding. 'Never,' he groaned. 'Never again. I swear to you, never again.'

David retrieved his bowler and left the shop.

Eight

Belinda burst into tears when she found that Tom was still at the flat. She fell into his arms. Here was the comforter she wanted. She could not conceive what she would have done if he had left for the pottery. He was wonderful. He did not ask a single question. The only time he perturbed her, by disengaging her arms from him, was to go and make a cup of tea. He brought it to her, heavily sugared, with one for himself, and held her again. She never wanted to move from this shelter.

'It was almost worth being attacked by Conrad to find you here,' she said at last, with a sniff and a half-laugh which showed she was recovering. He heard the whole story, felt moderately sorry for her, was bemused to find her depending on him. She was like a mother who suddenly announces that she is ill, in the touching faith that those she has looked after will now look after her, nurse her, bring her meals in bed, attend to the many and tedious chores she did. Belinda was quite sure he would help her.

He wanted to help her. But he had such an escapist temperament that he wondered how long he would be obliged to go on doing so. The answer might be to behave with extravagant tenderness towards her now, like the guest who, to create a good impression, even to quiet his own conscience, does all the washing up on the first night; having already, in secret, excused himself from further work.

Looking into her wonderful eyes, he caught a better side of himself, the one he tried to suppress as being sentimental. At that moment, he wanted to be tender, to find his happiness in making her happy. Knowing how weak he was, he fortified this love by reflecting what credit she would do him as a girlfriend.

'My God, you're lovely!' he exclaimed. 'As Peter Sellers would have said.'

She laughed more fluently. 'You're not so bad.'

'I love you!' He was agitated. He hadn't meant to say that.

She held his head, searching his face as though frightened. Tom felt uneasy. She must hear that he had struck a false note. He hoped so. To add a disclaimer would be too unkind. He couldn't say: 'I'm sorry, what I mean is I'm drawn to you, and amazed and proud that you're in my arms, and I want you to be happy. The words about loving you slipped out because I thought they were what you wanted to hear.'

Speech could have told her the truth, but his silence deceived her. She saw he was embarrassed. He must be thinking he had gone too far, that she could not return his love. He had reason enough. He was young and inexperienced and poor. He had not even learned how attractive he was to women.

'Don't be afraid,' she said softly. She leant forward and gave him a gentle kiss on the lips, a little girl's kiss. His stricken expression was, she thought, appropriate. They had been struck by lightning. She had not looked to fall in love with a twenty-four-year-old. As for him, he was attracted to her on the night of the dinner-party, but had no inkling that his desire would deepen into love. She kissed him again.

He was still constrained. She understood why. That morning she had been the victim of a sexual assault. She knew how difficult the boyfriend of a rape victim could find accepting what had occurred. Nothing so dreadful had

77

befallen her, but she had been distraught when she came home. Tom felt how agonizing a forceful approach by a man would be to her. It was strange to think that but for Conrad's vileness, she and Tom would have taken longer to become so close. Her suffering had driven them together. Poor Tom, it had been upsetting for him.

'Would you like some more tea?' her lodger asked. 'Actually, it's time you ate something. You must be hungry.' He knew he was.

She clung closer to him. The poor darling was in a state of shock. He didn't realize that she wanted him to come to bed. All at once she released him. 'I know!' she exclaimed. 'I bought something for you. Let's have it now.' He sat on the sofa with his head in his hands, wondering what to do. She was going mad. Either he went mad too, or they had a scene. He didn't want their affair to end so soon.

He heard her go into the kitchen, take something out of the fridge. She came back with an object wrapped in tissue paper and stood before him. Again he was reminded of a child, so entirely did she enter into what she was doing.

'This is for you,' she said, presenting it to him. It was heavy and cold in his hands. Pulling away the paper, he found a bottle of champagne.

'Do you want to drink it now?' he asked.

'Of course. I expect it's the best thing for shock.' She ran and fetched two glasses. He fumbled with the foil. 'Here, let me do it. I worked in a restaurant once.' She took it from him, tore off the foil, unwound the wire, held the neck of the bottle in one hand, the cork in the other, eased it out with a faint pop. A wisp of vapour drifted over the rim. The wine was frothing up. 'Quick,' he said. She raised a glass to catch it. 'That's because I shook it bringing it back last night,' she said, sounding gloriously pleased with herself. It had been an impulse buy on her way home to get changed for the party. 'I thought you'd see me bring it in but you didn't, so I hid it in the back of the fridge to be a surprise. Now you must propose a toast.'

'I want to drink to you, and to your escape, and to your kindness to me, which I don't deserve, and' – he faltered – 'and to my love for you.' The dryness of the champagne elated him. He did not see how a man could fail to love her, she was so sweet and beautiful. He was filled, at least, with something similar to love.

'And I want to drink to you. As soon as I met you in Wales I knew there was something between us.'

'I desired you then.'

'I know you did. I could tell by the way you looked at me. I thought it was cheeky.'

'If I were you, I'd have nothing to do with a cheeky young man.'

'I thought I'd better try to teach you some manners. If I didn't, who would? So I invited you to dinner.'

'My behaviour remained atrocious.'

'And the next day I came to lunch with you!' She laughed at her folly. 'I must already have been in love. How is it that you can fall in love so quickly? No, Tom. Stop.' He was trying to refill her glass. 'Let's save it for afterwards.' They wrestled with the bottle. He was taken aback by her determination.

'I want some now,' he protested. 'You gave it to me.'

'All right,' she said, having won. 'I'll pour you a little and put the rest in the fridge for afterwards.'

'One of the most overused words in the English language,' he said.

'What is?' she asked, embracing him over the back of the sofa, wishing he would hurry up and finish his drink.

'Afterwards. Later's pretty bad too. You've leafed through some book and at last you find a sex scene, and you've earned your reward for ploughing through all those pages, and you're looking forward to a detailed description, in which they do all sorts of things to each other, at the end of which his cock is filling her and soars up and up into her and her cries grow more and more frantic and they simultaneously explode; and instead you find the first word

79

of the next paragraph or chapter – people often screw between chapters – is afterwards.'

Afterwards they finished the bottle. (It was wonderful. His cock did soar up and up, etc. He knew exactly what to do.) Her lover said he was hungry. She told him to stay in bed and brought him some food, gleeful as if it were a midnight feast in the dorm.

'I was furious when Hamish turned against you because you're Jewish,' she said.

'There were other reasons.'

'Maybe, but a civilized person shouldn't give way to racism. Not that you look Jewish.'

He laughed. 'Hamish had less to go on.'

'You mean you aren't?'

'Do I look it?' He encouraged her to examine him. 'Coleman has been known to be a Jewish name, but in my case not. I'd quite like to be a Jew, except then I'd probably want to be Anglo-Saxon.'

'You're still a bit of a Vandal.' She disliked the ease with which he had lied to Hamish, though Hamish had asked for it. Or rather, she disliked being taken in herself. But she would not let this spoil her happiness. We are more inclined to dwell on our miseries than our happiness. Today she was happy and was going to recognize the fact.

In the middle of the afternoon she tried to get out of bed. He stopped her.

'Surely you remember from when you were a student that it's the best place to spend the afternoon?' he said.

'But there are things to do.' Even at university she had seldom spent the entire afternoon in bed.

'What?' His kiss stopped an answer. As their embrace tightened, she gave an expectant sigh.

'There's nothing to eat for supper,' she replied half an hour afterwards.

'We'll go out.'

'I'm sure there's something we ought to be getting on and doing.'

'This is our honeymoon,' he said. 'We can't work on our honeymoon.' An astute stroke: romance won her. 'Tomorrow we'll start work. Today we'll get in the right mood. We won't make the right decisions unless we're in the right mood. You mustn't go back to a world where the approval of Hamish and his mother is what matters. Don't you see they held you captive? Hamish is dominated by his mother, you're dominated by yours. You've no real independence at all.'

'I refused David.'

'In the end. And this morning you maybe think you did a brilliant thing as well, the equivalent of me refusing to work for my father's company and going to art college.'

'Who paid for that?'

'My mother, as a matter of fact. And the studio. But that's beside the point. You see, for you there was an alternative. Your boss fancied you, which isn't surprising. He could hardly have refused you a pay rise, if you'd thought of asking for one. As it was, he offered to make you a partner. He also wanted to have dinner with you, supposedly to fix this up, and even agreed that your boyfriend should be there. Conrad could have been persuaded to support the boyfriend, provided you went on being nice to him.

'But instead, at the first sign of sexual harassment, you slapped him across the face. How easy it would have been to give the man a kiss, tell him you could go no further and arrange a time for dinner. In the eyes of men, your strength is your sex appeal. You've turned it into a weakness. You dress so men fancy you, but when they do you run away, though all you've achieved is the desired effect.'

'I don't understand,' she said. 'You seem to be criticizing me for not taking advantage of Conrad on your behalf.'

'No, Bel.' He would not say the unworthy thought had crossed his mind this morning, before he decided to make the best of a bad job, give up the pottery, which was starting to bore him, and find something else to do. 'All I'm doing is admiring your courage. You were true to yourself. You didn't turn prostitute. Do you know my favourite verse in the Bible? "Take no thought for the morrow." You can only be true to yourself when you follow that commandment.'

'You'd better turn preacher,' she said. 'You're fluent enough.'

'I say whatever comes into my head.'

He was juvenile, she knew, but she loved him. Who said this was a mistake? When she considered the maturity of her contemporaries, she thought immaturity was worth trying.

Nine

'David has been arrested.'

'Hamish, is this one of your jokes?'

She and Tom had returned from an Indian restaurant in high spirits. There were two messages on her answering machine, both from Hamish. He said it was vital she telephone him as soon as she got back; repeated that it was of the greatest importance, as something terrible had happened. Tom thought the morning would do, but she said she would not be able to sleep until she had rung.

'It's not a joke,' Hamish said. 'It's deadly serious. He might have to leave the army.'

'How awful! But you haven't said what it's got to do with me.'

'Perhaps it would be better if you spoke to him direct.'

'I thought you said he'd been arrested.'

'He's out on police bail. We've been waiting for you to come back. He wanted to come round to your flat and wait for you there, but I persuaded him it would be better to stay with me and Ann-Louise.' They had spent a hellish evening holding David in check. 'Here he is.'

'Belinda?'

'Hello, David. I'm sorry to hear you've been arrested.'

'The whole thing is impossible to explain on the telephone. What I need to do is come and see you.'

'It's rather late.'

'I can get to you in a quarter of an hour. Look, I'll just jump in a cab.'

'Don't do that. Surely you can give me some idea on the phone of what's happened?'

'You know your employer Conrad Smith assaulted you this morning?'

'Who told you that? I'm not sure it could really be called an assault. I expect I over-reacted. Anyway, I feel better now it's happened. I can't think how I stuck working more than a day for him.' She was too good at enduring unsatisfactory situations.

'I was passing your gallery this afternoon and called in on the off chance of seeing you, and was told by your colleague what had happened, having promised her I wouldn't tell Smith she'd told me.'

'She can't have given you a very good description. She wasn't in the room.'

'It was enough.' David felt uncomfortable, not only because Belinda was being unhelpful, but because he did not know how to relate his dealings with Smith without seeming to brag. 'I was incensed by his treatment of you, as any friend of yours would have been.'

'I think I gave as good as I got. The door must have given him a nasty bang when I went out, and I'd already hit him across the face. I'm not totally incapable of looking after myself.'

'All the same, you can imagine how I felt. I wanted to tell Smith what I thought of him.' Belinda recalled that Tom had shown no interest in telling Conrad what he thought of him. 'So I waited a few minutes to see whether he'd come back, and at 5.30 he did. He mistook me for your boyfriend. Assured me he'd buy a large number of table-lamps from me.'

David had not intended to put that in, but she had heard his story so far with such calmness that he had to mention it. He needed it all to matter to her. It was easier to talk to her than to Hamish and Ann-Louise. He wanted her to sympathize with every detail. Besides, the legal ramifications of the affair justified telling the story in full.

'So I heard what the wretched Smith had to say for himself,' he went on, 'and then I hit him.'

'Because he thought you were my boyfriend?'

'Don't be silly. Because of what he'd done to you. He claimed there'd been a misunderstanding between you and him, but I could see he knew quite well that he was in the wrong. He deserved everything he got. The thing is, he was a bit slow to promise not to do it again, so he finished up in rather a mess.'

'Oh, David.'

'I walked out of the shop and someone said: "Excuse me, sir." I had no idea I was being addressed until I bumped into a policeman. He'd stepped right in front of me. I apologized to him, thinking it was an accident, but he asked me to come back into the shop. At first I refused. He looked like a corporal of horse I once had, and I was damned if I was going to let him order me about. Then he arrested me.'

'Good God!'

'He cautioned me that anything I said might be taken down and used in evidence against me, then he said that if I didn't come quietly, he'd handcuff me. He also radioed for reinforcements, as though I was a dangerous criminal. I saw I had no option but to go back into the shop.

'Smith was sitting up against the wall. His nose was bleeding, but as far as I could see he wasn't in bad shape. He took a turn for the worse when he saw the policeman, started to snivel and fell over on his side. The copper gabbled some more into his radio, requesting an ambulance. I suggested Smith pull himself together, which didn't go down too well. Another policeman and a policewoman arrived, and the ambulance crew, and after a while the police constable who'd arrested me said I must accompany him to the station.

'I said that was ridiculous, as I had a perfectly good explanation, but he replied that it would be better for all concerned if we tape-recorded what I had to say in accordance with the provisions of the Police and Criminal Evidence Act. So off we went in one of their cars. They were perfectly correct in the form of words they used to address me, at least for most of the time, but thoroughly insolent in their manner. At the station, a sergeant booked me in – they were interested to find out what I did – and I had to hand over the contents of my pockets. I'd already demanded to speak to my solicitor, but they said I couldn't until these formalities were over. After that I got given a piece of paper saying I could ring him. Fortunately he was still at his office, and was able to come straight round. He wanted to send a colleague who specializes in criminal work, but he wasn't available. Meanwhile the police told me to take off my shoes, in case I tried to commit suicide, and locked me in a cell. This was meant to soften me up, I think, but it made me angrier.

'Eventually my solicitor arrived, a chap called Henry Meredith whose father looked after my father. Up to that point, I thought the whole performance could be put down to an over-zealous constable who happened to be passing the shop and didn't understand what was going on. Once Henry had heard the PC's version of events, he came to see me. I said that Conrad Smith had behaved in a monstrous way to you, and been unable to give a satisfactory account of his behaviour, so I hit him. Henry replied that this was no defence. You were not allowed to hit someone because the person in question had maltreated a friend of yours. If I'd hit Smith, I'd have to plead guilty.

'I was staggered. It was so completely obvious that I was in the right, I couldn't imagine pleading guilty. Henry said if it could be shown that the victim had molested you, and that you were a friend of mine, we could enter a plea of mitigation, and since it was the first offence, I would probably get off with a fine, or even a conditional discharge. I pointed out that this was no comfort, for I should certainly have to resign my commission, so my career was ruined.

'He said that if there was a suitable moment, he would try to persuade the police that the episode was a one-off mistake which would devastate my career if it came to trial. If I was incredibly lucky, they might let me off with a caution. But he thought the victim's attitude was crucial. If Smith could be persuaded not to give evidence against me, the police were much less likely to go ahead. Henry had been told, however, that they'd already got a statement from Smith, which we'd be given a copy of, saying I assaulted him. I pointed out that if Smith could talk, his injuries were not serious, but Henry said once the flesh was broken, as Smith's certainly was, a charge of grievous bodily harm could be brought. If I'd only bruised him, it would have been actual bodily harm. If it had been what they call common assault, i.e. just threats, the police probably wouldn't have bothered. The police constable had arrived on the scene just as I threw Smith on the floor at the end, and hadn't witnessed the rest of the assault.

'So the question is, how can we bring pressure to bear on Smith? If Smith thought he was going to face an assault charge himself, he might be persuaded to withdraw his own statement, though the police wouldn't be too friendly to him if he tried to do that. I asked Henry if he could go and see Smith, but he said that was out of the question. Apparently it would amount to tampering with witnesses.'

'I see why you needed to talk to me,' Belinda said.

'After Henry and I had conferred, he accompanied me to a room where they tape-recorded the evidence. The police constable only wanted an admission of guilt. He wasn't interested in my motives. At the end, when he asked me if I had anything else to say, Henry said I should explain why I acted so out of character, and I said I had reason to believe that earlier in the day, the victim had assaulted a female member of his staff who was a close friend of mine. He didn't ask me how close.'

'The whole thing is too much to take in,' she said.

87

'I told you it would be better if I could come round, but if that's not possible, it's not possible.'

'Dear David, I'm afraid it isn't possible tonight. I'm sorry.' They were transported back over their relationship, she to feeling for him even as she denied him, he to a vast effort when the conversation was finished to draw from her scanty remarks what shreds of comfort, or proofs of hopelessness, he could. 'Dear David': that showed affection. 'It isn't possible tonight': that showed there was someone more important than himself, whom she would not put aside even when he was in terrible difficulties.

It might not be anyone special: in a way, that would make it worse. Or it might be the potter-boyfriend, whoever he was. Hamish and Ann-Louise had been embarrassed when he said that Smith had mistaken him for a potter. She said, as if it was funny, that she'd never seen a potter in a bowler hat. In her absence, Hamish might have been more informative. David wouldn't put the question direct. He abhorred the thought of spying on her. He only wanted to know if someone was exploiting her; was not sure he could stand hearing that a normal, pleasant fellow was enjoying her love.

'Henry's going to hand the case over to a colleague called Michael Chan, the chap who couldn't come to the station. I've spoken to Chan already. He wondered if you could come and see him at ten tomorrow morning, or else phone to fix another time.'

'Of course I'll come. Tell me where to be. I do want to help.' Her guilt at his suffering came to the surface. She had been so mean. She held his happiness in her power and did not give it; could at least try to be nicer to him, instead of demanding the one bleak sacrifice of his absence.

When the call was over, she found her ear lobe was hurting. She must have been pressing the receiver against it. She rubbed it, hardly aware that Tom had come to sit beside her.

'What was that all about?' he asked.

She summarized what David had said.

'I hope he apologized.'

'No,' she said. 'Why should he?'

'For being an interfering bastard.'

'He thought he was standing up for me.'

'It was none of his business. He should leave you alone. He didn't even know what had happened. If anyone was going to intervene, it should have been me. I'd heard what went on between you and Conrad, and I could see you'd given as good as you got, and that it would only lead to further hassle if I went round to beat him up.'

She would not have minded if Tom had said he wanted to beat Conrad up, though she would have stopped him. 'David was terribly unlucky to be caught,' she said.'I should think the chances of a policeman walking past the gallery at that moment and seeing what was going on were about a million to one.'

'Let's face it,' Tom said. 'Sooner or later he was going to get caught. He sounds psychopathic. Putting him behind bars mightn't be a bad idea, especially as it doesn't take long to see who his next target will be. I'm definitely going to give up pottery. If he comes round here asking "Where's the potter?" I'll say "Couldn't tell you, guv. I'm in video rentals."'

'You don't understand.'

Women often told you that. 'Look, Bel, you haven't thought this through. David's case is going to get into the papers. I can see it now: "GALLOPING MAJOR AVENGES BLONDE WHO SPURNED HIM. Lovelorn Major David Cheney punched the man who dared to lay a finger on his former girlfriend, beautiful Belinda Gould, a court in London heard yesterday. The horse-mad Major, a member of the élite Household Cavalry who guard the Queen and other members of the Royal Family, saw red when a shop assistant told him Belinda had gone home early after she was the victim of a sexual attack by her employer, South African-born designer Conrad Smith." It's got everything for the tabloids: sex, violence, royalty, pictures of you looking seductive and the Galloping Major on horseback looking violent. "Friends revealed that the couple had been very close when Old Etonian David was stationed in London and Windsor, but that when he was posted to Zimbabwe Belinda said the relationship must end."'

'None of my friends would talk to the press about me.'

'I never would, but can you be sure about everybody? Think how interesting your story will be for them. They'll all be talking about it at their boring dinner-parties, and then items will get into the diary columns, and it only takes one person to ring up the *Sun* for them to have their exclusive. They'll all do background pieces. If they don't know anything else, they'll embroider what was said in court, and if they do know more they'll embroider that too. They'll stake this place out and get snatch pictures of you walking to your car. You ought to find an agent, then you could make a lot of money. Why not make me your agent? You could be the new Pamella Bordes. The best line I read about her was by one of her so-called friends: "Pamella always accepted that lingerie was an investment." Classic. We'll have the Major showering you with gifts of erotic underwear. "Belinda never had to buy her own suspender belts. She could always rely on the Major to keep her supplied." How many MPs have you had? Pity Hamish hasn't been elected. We can always use the "unknown Cabinet Minister" ploy. We'll stockpile plenty of glamour pictures to feed into the papers at each stage of the story.'

'You've got a perverted mind.' She wept in silence. Tom had seemed so innocent, yet his mind was stuffed with junk films, junk books, junk newspapers. He was like someone out of a Martin Amis novel. He said she couldn't imagine what the trial would be like, but she could see it all. She hated standing up in front of people and saying things. After university she wondered whether to be a primary-school teacher, and decided she couldn't because she knew what an ordeal facing a class of children would be; let alone a court; let alone talking about her sex life.

He had the effrontery to put his arm round her. 'I'm only trying to warn you,' he said. 'I assume that even with your penchant for self-sacrifice you won't be insane enough to bring a case against Conrad, but if you do it will be worse. The prosecution will try to suggest you led him on. They'll ask who wanted to have this meeting in his little room. What were you wearing? Did you know your knees would be touching? Were you not a designing woman who lured him on because you wanted him to buy your boyfriend's pottery?'

'Shut up,' she shouted. 'I can't take any more of your babytalk.'

He waited a while. 'I'm sorry, Bel. It's only that I'm jealous of David.'

'You've no reason to be jealous, you foolish boy.'

'You're tired.'

'I just want to try to go to sleep.'

'I'll sleep in the other bedroom if it would be better for you.' He'd get some peace.

'You can stay with me as long as you don't take all the duvet.' At three in the morning, when he was breathing noisily beside her and she could not sleep, she wanted to chuck him out, but hadn't the heart to wake him.

Ten

Belinda arrived on the stroke of ten at the offices of Gandon and Gandon, solicitors, in a street just the other side of Oxford Street from Mayfair. The firm did not look a grand one: she recalled David saying that the Cheneys kept their money by avoiding grandeur, not even buying a title. She wore a grey flannel jacket and skirt, a white blouse. Tom had mocked her for looking like a solicitor. The good thing about him was that he always reacted.

Someone showed her up to Michael Chan's room. His manner was extravagantly English. He had the romantic love of his adopted country which native Englishmen were too undemonstrative to express. When did an Englishman last tell you his country is marvellous? Michael could talk with wonder of his schooldays at Harrow, his outings to Newmarket, his tailor, his clubs, his boat. He relished these things, and told you about them, not in order to prove a social point, but out of genuine pleasure. The moroseness of English life escaped him.

'Miss Gould,' he said, grinning. 'Please come in. Here is a chair. My room is poky, I'm afraid. I am, you see, the criminal partner in a firm devoted to wills and trusts and other family matters. They gave the Chinaman the grubby end of the business.' He laughed with delight. 'Magistrates' courts. Police cells. That sort of thing. Not that I wish to convey a lack of sympathy for your friend Major Cheney's plight. It is unenviable. Would you care for a cigarette? These are Turkish.'

He held out a silver cigarette case. Amused by the anachronism, she took one.

'Now that, you see, was a trick, for I hope you will stay until you have finished it. But strictly speaking, you can leave now. Major Cheney asked me to inform you that he has had a change of heart since last night. He has decided he does not wish to put any pressure on Conrad Smith. He is simply going to plead guilty. Having slept on the matter, he is determined that you should not be involved in any way whatever. I apologize. I tried to telephone you at home to tell you not to come, but you had already left.'

'But this is ridiculous,' she said. 'If I understood what he told me, his only hope is to do a deal for Conrad to drop the charge against him and me to drop the charge against Conrad.'

'My instructions, acting as I am for Major Cheney, are to tell you that he has resolved, and resolved unshakeably, that you should have no part whatever to play in his case. He added that he did not wish to discuss the matter further with you; asked me to apologize for troubling you.'

'Very well, Mr Chan. Our business is over.'

'I'm afraid it is, Miss Gould.'

'So now, I hope, I can talk to you as a friend. I don't suppose I could afford to talk to you as a client anyway. Is that little boy your son?'

'My son and heir,' the solicitor said, picking up the photograph on his desk. 'He is wearing the uniform of his prep school, a fine establishment in Berkshire. But Miss Gould, I am afraid they do not do enough Latin.'

'I was rotten at Latin.'

'So was I! So was I!' He let out a peal of laughter. 'But how can one take a school seriously where they do not study the classics? It is a contradiction in terms. When I go to take Freddie out, I tell the headmaster: more Latin! As for Greek, they do not learn the alphabet. But Freddie does

93

not want Latin or Greek. He enjoys computers. Miss Gould, please, if you ever send a boy to prep school, remember to ask about Latin.'

'I promise you I will, but since I have no children I want to ask you about something else. If I did wish to put pressure on Conrad Smith, what would I do?'

'Miss Gould —'

'Belinda.'

'Belinda, I'm not sure I can answer that question. It really would be best if you went to see your own solicitor. If I were him, mind you, I might only be hinting at the answer. In fact, I would probably advise you to do as Major Cheney asks.'

'You're not my solicitor. I haven't even got a solicitor. All I've ever needed is conveyancing and my father's firm did that, and I don't want to talk to them. I thought you'd help me. I had a long affair with David. I should have ended it sooner, as I couldn't feel as much for him as he did for me. But when he told me about the arrest I wanted to help him. He was terribly unfortunate to be seen by a policeman.'

'Most unfortunate.'

'I'm sure I know why he changed his mind last night. He suddenly regretted having troubled me. The whole point of his intervention was to protect me, not to expose me to the horrors of a trial and its coverage in the press. His duty was to spare me at whatever cost to himself. He must resign his commission and plead guilty, without even entering a plea of mitigation. I know him. He'll instruct you to say nothing about me to the court. The assault will remain without motive, so his punishment will be heavier. He'd rather go to prison than admit he hit Conrad because Conrad molested me. People laugh at David. I've laughed at him, and I know his motives are mixed, but he means what he says. His belief that a man must protect a woman sounds absurd to most people, but he acts on it. His idea of honour is no more fashionable than your insistence on Latin.'

94

'He is a rescuer of the damsel in distress,' Michael Chan said, getting rather carried away.

'I'm terrified of being attacked.'

'Did Conrad Smith leave no mark on you?'

She took off her jacket, rolled up her sleeve. A bruise had appeared on her upper arm where Conrad's fingers had dug into it.

Michael removed a camera from a drawer of his desk. 'If you will turn your arm so that the flash catches the worst of it, I will immortalize this outrage. We should have your face in some of these.'

'Actual bodily harm,' she said.

'You make my knowledge redundant. You could tell Mr Smith you will try to persuade the police to charge him, and if that fails, you will bring a complaint yourself. Is it too much to hope he marked you elsewhere?'

'I gave him no chance.'

'I ought to warn you that you have little chance of success. Major Cheney has forbidden me to intercede with the police superintendent who will decide whether or not to pass the case to the Crown Prosecution Service. Otherwise I would have tried to persuade him that my client should be let off with a caution. The superintendent knows I don't push my luck, but I doubt I would have influenced him this time. He has the defendant's clear admission of guilt. It will be a success to put in the crime figures.'

'You mustn't tell David that I might try to talk to Conrad.'

'Certainly not. You came here, I gave you my client's message, you went away. Our talk would be better left unmentioned to anyone. Let me give you this roll of film. Let me also implore you to be careful. If you have to meet Conrad Smith, you do promise me you will do so in a public place?'

'But of course,' she said. 'Thank you very much for your help.'

Eleven

Cedric Williams already looked thinner when Hamish visited him in hospital.

'I can hardly swallow,' he explained. 'They're still not sure what's the matter. At first they thought it was heart. Well, it is heart. I had a heart attack before they brought me in here. Total collapse, death's door, three days in intensive care. But there are other symptoms, including this trouble swallowing, which I've had a month or two but it's got worse. They say it might be reflux oesophagitis.'

Hamish wondered whether it was cancer.

'I expect you're wondering whether it's cancer,' Cedric said.

'Oh no.'

'I asked them. They said they didn't know yet. They've got to shove this tube down my throat to find out. An endoscopy, it's called. They have a look through it. The chap in the bed over there says that if they don't like what they see, they do a bioscopy next, to get hold of a piece of tissue. At least that's what they did to him. Then they told him he'd got cancer.'

'But you've always been so fit,' Hamish protested.

'I haven't, actually. I'm overweight. Being a bachelor, I haven't looked after myself. Half the constituency association think I'm gay.'

Hamish tried to look surprised.

'They'll reckon AIDS is finishing me off. Do I strike you as an AIDS patient?'

'No.'

'It's an unfair question, really. I don't expect you've met an AIDS patient.'

'Not as far as I'm aware.'

'I wish I had got AIDS. It would be one in the eye for my association. How they'd feel the shame. Ah, you're shocked now.'

'No, no.'

'You're not being very assertive, Hamish.'

'I suppose not.'

'None of my visitors has dared contradict a word I say. They think I couldn't stand it, but what about them? All they want to hear is good news, or news they can give a cheerful spin to. "It's wonderful you're out of intensive care," they say, as if it wasn't much worse that I ever went in. They consider it in poor taste if I mention cancer. It forces them to say: "Well, there's a lot they can do for you these days." One of my colleagues in the House who came and saw me said he'd read an article in the *Independent* by a retired doctor who was dying of cancer, riddled with secondary growths, the physicians all despaired of him but some well-wisher persuaded this fellow to go on a diet consisting of nothing but pulses. Do you know what a pulse is?'

'Not really.'

'Neither do I. Anyhow, needless to say the retired doctor made a complete recovery. He's spent most of the time since his illness water-skiing or whatever. Thinking up new recipes for pulses probably. My colleague couldn't remember whether one can revert to steak and kidney pudding after the treatment, but I expect you feel so well you don't want to. There's only one aspect of the story which I find hard to credit.'

'Oh yes, what's that?'

'Why should any Conservative Member of Parliament want to read the *Independent*?'

Hamish gave a poor imitation of a chuckle, to avoid admitting he shared the conventional view that the *Independent* was rather a good newspaper.

'Maybe his wife showed him the article,' Cedric speculated. 'If I had a wife I loved, I might read articles about pulses. I'd also feel less demob happy. Assuming this illness is fatal, it'll be like breaking up early from school. I'm fifty-seven, but I know I look nearer seventy. The end is nigh. Three cheers for the holidays, as the headmaster used to say. You can tell the ward sister my mind's wandering. When I lie in this bed, I realize I haven't much liked the last twenty years. I never got anywhere in Parliament. Stuck on the backbenches. Not even asked to become someone's private secretary. Frankly, I never had much to say. I had my food and drink and I've tried to tell jokes, in order not to be a burden on my friends. They claim not to be tired of my company, but I am. I'm fed up with it.'

'Oh dear,' Hamish said.

'I'm not looking for sympathy. I'm trying to explain why I feel pretty bobbish, as my grandmother used to say. You'd ask her how she was and she'd reply "pretty bobbish". But I'm wasting your time. You're not here to collect material for *The Life and Times of Cedric Williams MP*. You want to find out how to get my seat.'

'Well, that is to say –'

'Find somewhere else. They're a troublesome lot.'

'I enjoyed coming to speak at your dinner.'

'We enjoyed having you, dear boy. But have you ever known your fascinating little talk on modern industrial society's need for a well-trained workforce, adorned, if I recall, with quotations from Burke and Disraeli, lead to questions entirely about immigration?'

'My belief is that racial tensions are much better incorporated within the Conservative Party,' Hamish began, 'where they can be safely directed, than allowed to fester in fringe groups of the far right, whose members grow resentful that they are denied parliamentary representation. England for

98

the English: that must always be true. But remember that Burke was from Ireland and Disraeli, one of the Tory Party's greatest Prime Ministers, was, like Jesus Christ, a Jew. We can absorb a certain number of foreigners. Numbers, however, are of the essence, and I myself would deprecate any further net immigration from the New Commonwealth. If there are people who have come here, and find they are unhappy, every assistance should be given to enable them to return home. But remember, while they are here, they enjoy the same rights as each one of us, neither more nor less.'

'You'll lose your audience in that last sentence. The bits which show you're not a racist have to be carefully packaged for my association.'

'Neither more nor less. And that is where we must say to the Muslims in our country: enough is enough. We all know Salman Rushdie is a rotten novelist. We are only too well aware that Rugby failed to teach him the rudiments of manners or of English grammar. How much more benefit, one may say in passing, P. G. Wodehouse derived from his schooldays at Dulwich College. But nevertheless, for an Ayatollah in Persia to take exception to Rushdie's unreadable work and pronounce a death sentence on him is behaviour which the British Government cannot be expected to condone. Were the Pope to do such a thing, we could not and would not stand idly by. No more can we, or have we, or will we ever in a thousand years, stand idly by when a Muslim tries to ignore the due processes of British law. All British Muslims must demonstrate that their first loyalty is to this country, not to some oriental bigot.'

'You might pass muster with that. "Swamp" is a useful word, as in "I think we all worry sometimes that we may be swamped". Capital punishment?'

'Glorious pinnacle of our judicial system. Terrible loss. Bring back the rope, first of all for terrorists and for people who murder police officers. Not yet convinced we need it for domestic murders: no proof of deterrent effect: all know

99

how annoying the family can be, heat of moment, etc.'

'I wouldn't risk any lighter touches, if I were you. You may have a chance. You won't intimidate them intellectually, though you must lay off the child's history of Conservative thought. Socially, you're wrong. Toff's mannerisms. Buy a polyester tie. I can't remember if you're married.'

'Engaged.'

'You'll have to take her along. They don't want to make the same mistake they did with me.'

The ward sister had come to stand at the foot of the bed. 'You've had long enough,' she said to Hamish.

'Goodbye,' the patient said. 'I tell you what, I'll write to Victor. He's the leader of the moderates, has his own reasons for wanting to get in with Central Office. The party, of course, will be anxious to stop an out-and-out racist from grabbing the nomination. I'll tell him he could run you as the respectable candidate against the Hitler Youth.'

'Thank you,' the respectable candidate said as he was guided away. 'I hope you get better soon.'

'Pop in next week if you've time. At this rate of shrinkage, I should start looking younger.'

On the way out, Hamish met Maureen, Cedric's secretary from the House of Commons, bringing in the mail. They spent a couple of minutes chatting.

'Cedric was in such good form he even said he was going to write a letter about me,' Hamish remarked.

'I expect he'll want me to take it down,' she said. 'Don't worry about it.'

'I don't think he believes he's going to die,' Hamish reported to Ann-Louise. 'He's developed a fantasy in which he doesn't mind dying because he doesn't think he will.'

'Maybe he won't.'

'If he does, I don't really want the seat. To succeed him at the next general election would be all right, but it'll be a fiendish by-election. The majority's 13,000, which isn't enough. Cedric said the association are a frightful lot, much given to squabbling among themselves, but he's going to write to someone called Victor, proposing me as a moderate.'

'One can, I suppose, get back to civilization quite soon. I mean it's near to London.'

'You poor darling, you still don't want me to be a politician, do you.'

'I don't see why you shouldn't have your own interests as long as they don't involve me. My mother's career was ruined because Daddy's in the Foreign Office and dragged her all over the world. The year she was meant to take her exams Daddy was posted to Islamabad and I arrived. Since then she's been celebrating the Queen's birthday and trying to make friends with the other wives.'

To hear Ann-Louise reiterate this view depressed Hamish. He thought a loyal wife should give her husband the help he needed in whatever career he had chosen; find her satisfaction by sharing in his successes, consoling him in his failures, giving dinner-parties for his colleagues, having a meal ready when he came back late at night, looking after their children. The last task was far more important and interesting than any career a man might have. Ann-Louise, however, said she intended to have a nanny and go back to the law. Hamish hoped that when the time came she would think again. She was very young. She did not realize how maternal she would feel, nor how exhausted she would get trying to be a lawyer as well as a mother. Nor did she understand the difficulty of finding satisfactory help. It was unsettling for infants to be passed from one New Zealander to another every few months.

'Your mother seems fairly happy,' he observed.

'Well, she oughtn't to be,' Ann-Louise said, annoyed by his obtuseness. She would win, for she had ten times his determination, but educating him would be tedious. He was like a large teddy bear. Once you had played with him for a bit, it was difficult to think of anything else to do with him.

'Whereas Belinda's unhappy because she hasn't got married,' he said.

'Then why don't you bloody well make her happy by marrying her?' He was bewildered. 'Aren't you a silly little Hamster?' she said, rubbing his tummy. She could be the nasty interrogator and the nice interrogator rolled into one. He gathered from the hand on his tummy that she was now being nice.

'Dearest Antelope,' he ventured. She pulled the grey hairs on the side of his head through her fingers. That was a sign of affection. When she had begun calling him Hamster he greatly disliked the name, but thought he should reciprocate. His first idea was Ant, but she might not wish to be so small, so he settled on Antelope.

'Do you think I'm an anteloper?' she asked.

'I don't know. What do antelopers do?'

'They prey on young hamsters who want to be Tory MPs, undermine their ideas and don't show how fond they are of them.'

'You sound the archetypal anteloper. It doesn't make Hamster any less fond of you. It keeps him on his toes. Hamster wants to stay with his paws round Antelope for ever and ever and ever.'

Twelve

After she had seen Michael Chan, Belinda left his roll of film at a shop promising a two-hour development service and looked for a public telephone. She wanted a quiet kiosk that would take a card, not money. The one she chose was covered in advertisements for prostitutes.

She got straight through to Conrad.

'How are you?' she asked.

'Lucky not to be dead.'

'Thank God you're alive.'

'No thanks to the maniac you sent to assassinate me. If it wasn't for my all-round physique, he might have stood a chance. As it was, he can be thankful I didn't use some moves I learnt with the South African Defence Force. All of us did unarmed combat. You might like to pass that on.'

'I promise you I didn't send him.'

'That makes no odds. He's going to pay for what he did. Boy is he going to pay. If his lawyers don't offer me satisfactory compensation, he can expect a civil suit for damages, loss of earnings, personal distress, the works. Once he's been convicted on the criminal charge there shouldn't be any problem about that. I suppose he got you to ring me up and try to talk me out of it? Tell him from me he's wasting his time.'

'You do sound tough, Conrad.'

'I guess I am kind of tough. My military service hardened me.'

'I remember your descriptions.' He could bore for the southern hemisphere on the feats of physical endurance he had performed as a conscript. By his own account, Conrad was very much a man's man, the type who could carry a rifle and ninety pounds of kit across the Kalahari Desert with only dried meat for sustenance. 'If Major Cheney had asked me before he tried to visit me,' Belinda went on, 'I'd have told him not to come near you. But he didn't consult me then, and he hasn't asked me to telephone you since. In fact, he'd be furious if he knew I was talking to you now.'

'Then tell the Major from me to go to hell. If you want to talk to me, you talk to me, and that's final.'

'I do want to talk to you, but it's not easy on the telephone to say the things I need to say. Things about you and me, Conrad.'

'You mean you've realized you were a bit thoughtless. Well, it looks like the whole world's going to take advantage of me this week. I let the Major down pretty lightly so I guess I'm prepared to do the same for you. As I recall, we were discussing dinner when you got so unreasonable. If you want to make it up with me, you can come and have dinner tonight.'

'Which restaurant would you like to go to?'

'A delightful little joint known as My Flat.'

'I couldn't put you to the trouble of cooking. I'd much rather go to the Gay Hussar.' She named the first place that came into her head. A friend had taken her there a few weeks ago and she liked it tremendously.

'You know, Belinda, that doesn't sound quite my kind of place, if you know what I mean.'

'It's in Greek Street,' she said, hoping Soho would appeal to Conrad. She could imagine him creeping round the streets after dark.

'And we don't need reminding what the Greeks got up to. Not my idea of fun at all. As for cooking, you would not believe what I can do to a steak. It's going to be a pleasure to entertain you *chez moi*.'

'What I'd really like is for me to entertain you.'

'You mean you'd rather I came over to your place?'

'I'll take you somewhere.'

'Out of the kindness of my heart I offer you dinner at my flat. That's the final offer. There are clients with me, so just say yes or no.'

'All right.'

She'd let the conversation get entirely out of hand. Dinner had advantages – the longer she spent with Conrad, the more optimistic she was that she could talk him round – but going to his flat should have been out of the question. Michael Chan said she must meet him in a public place. She should have been tougher. She was no good at threats.

Tom would be waiting for her to ring. She had promised to do so as soon as she was through at the lawyer's, but it was past noon. How could she explain that David wanted her to do nothing, but she was going to be out tonight? To the right of the telephone was a hand-written note, 'Busty Belinda', with a number. In the spirit of people who look over cliffs and wonder what it would be like to jump off, she considered crossing out the number and writing in her own. The idea seemed no worse than the prospect of dinner in Conrad's flat.

Someone tapped on the glass. She looked up and saw a man holding his hand to his ear. Withdrawing her card, she put it into her handbag and stepped outside. The kiosk was somewhere between Oxford Street and Grosvenor Square. She used to work near here, at a secretarial agency just off New Bond Street; turned in that direction.

It was strange that she had not thought before how she was going to earn a living. She wanted to broach the subject with Tom yesterday afternoon, but he had deflected her with his talk of a honeymoon. This morning she might have tried to get him to face facts, but the business of David and

Conrad intervened. Now she was using that to drive out fear of her own future.

Usually she thought about money a lot. She never had enough. Her mortgage was much too big for her income: she needed a lodger to help pay it, but had recently lost one. Her car, clothes and a small amount of entertaining all seemed to eat cash. While she had never been more than a glorified secretary, many of her friends were well-set in their careers, getting richer by the minute. She shared their tastes: when they came to dinner, she wanted them to have the same sort of food and drink as they offered her. She liked giving people good presents and having well-made things for herself. If she went into a shop where the prices were not displayed, four times out of five she preferred the more expensive version of something.

On leaving with the smart carrier bag containing her purchase, she would tell herself that in the long term you saved money by going for quality. Even good soap lasted twice as long as cheap stuff. Yet she was permanently behind with her bills and unable to live without an overdraft. At the moment it amounted to a month or so's salary, which was the maximum her bank, aware of her relative poverty, would tolerate. She could forget about this month's salary, which Conrad would have paid at the end of the week. Her next mortgage payment was due the week after and she owed about two months' salary on her credit cards.

Asking her parents for help was unthinkable. They had less and less spare cash themselves. She was able to keep afloat so long as she had a job, a lodger and no gaps between.

Instead, she was without a job and had acquired a live-in lover who had no visible means of support.

It was nevertheless with a feeling of virtue that she turned towards the secretarial agency. It showed forethought, to go there before imminent bankruptcy filled her mind with panic. She was not yet imagining, as she had during smaller financial crises in the past, the repossession of her flat by the building society, the difficulty of finding anywhere to store her possessions, the humiliation of a penniless return to Yorkshire.

If her friend Lindy had no longer been at the agency, she would have walked out again. 'Long time no see!' her former colleague said with a smile.

'I didn't even know whether you still worked here,' Belinda said, smiling herself.

'Not for much longer. I was just going to lunch. Shall we go together?'

Theirs had been the kind of friendship that can flourish at a place of work without extending beyond it. Each heard about the other's life in daily instalments, as one might listen to a long-running serial on the radio, taking a keen interest in the characters but not expecting to meet them. At most Lindy exchanged a word or two with a man who had come to see Belinda, or transferred a telephone call; Belinda, less often, doing the same for her. Friendship is sometimes the great consolation of an office or factory where the work is dull. Their talk had the added attraction that their social circles at no point overlapped. Lindy's father was a track worker for British Rail: Belinda remembered being struck by the fact that when Lindy was small, her mother took her once a week to the public baths because they had no bathroom at home.

'What's your news?' Belinda asked as they made their way to a sandwich bar.

'I'm getting married!' This had been the aspiration of Lindy's life, and, less explicitly, of Belinda's; not the only aim, but the one whose emotional importance could not be overstated. Belinda was sorry to affront progressive opinion by longing for her wedding day, but she could not help it.

Seated in the back of the sandwich bar, she heard about Lindy's husband. Arthur had set up some years ago in the wastepaper business, was doing well and wanted his wife to stop work at once in order to start a family. In his photograph, he wore an engaging grin. His fiancée looked ecstatic, lunching on an orange so she would get into her wedding dress. Belinda had never seen her so happy. She knew how depressed Lindy had been by her love life, or for long stretches by her lack of one. Now the radiant bride was describing what her bridesmaids would wear.

'But I mustn't hog the conversation,' she said. 'Tell me about yourself.'

'My life's rather complicated at the moment.' When they had worked together, sitting at their desks trying to fit the girls on their books to the vacancies notified by employers, the multiplicity of Belinda's suitors had excited Lindy's admiration. The contrast was now less favourable. It was this, not envy, which made Belinda feel sad. 'I haven't found my Arthur,' she added.

'You will.' Lindy wanted everyone to share her happiness. 'Are you in love?'

'I think so, but not with anyone I could marry.'

'You mean he's married already?'

'No. He's much younger than me and he hasn't even settled to a career. His name's Tom. Actually I wondered if you could do something for me.'

'Of course I will.'

'If Tom rings you tomorrow, tell him that I've spent this evening at your place, discussing whether I could come back and work for the agency.'

'I could tell him you're interested in my job. I'll be leaving in June. But surely you don't want it?'

'Maybe I ought to tell someone where I'm going tonight, if it's not a burden to you.'

Lindy tried to argue Belinda out of the plan. If David himself wanted her to do nothing, there was no possible reason why she should put herself at risk. If she must do something, she should persuade David first.

'That would be hopeless. I don't know why, but it's just because he's so determined I shouldn't do anything for him that I want to. Otherwise he's a pest.'

'Give me Conrad Smith's address and telephone number.

If you haven't rung by 10.30 to say you're all right, Arthur and I'll come and collect you.'

They had a further dispute about the time. Belinda said she would telephone by midnight, and would that afternoon entrust all but the best two photographs of her bruised arm to Lindy's safekeeping, though neither was quite clear how that would help.

'What if you haven't rung me?'

'I will have.'

After lunch she phoned Tom, with apologies for failing to do so earlier. She had feared he would be cross, but he did not mind. She told him David had sent a message that he did not want her to be involved, so finding herself near her old agency, she had gone in and begun negotiations about a job. She was meeting Lindy after work and having dinner with her to discuss it further.

'Good idea,' he said. 'I think at least one of us should earn something.'

Thirteen

The lift up to Conrad's flat was slow, an old thing of dark brown wood and black metal. He lived at the top of a mansion block in Ashley Gardens, next to Westminster Cathedral. As Belinda ascended, she told herself that most of the things one dreaded did not prove so bad. When she was invited to parties as a child, and had a sinking feeling of reluctance to leave her own house, her mother would say to her, 'You'll enjoy it when you get there', and usually she did. She could not expect to enjoy tonight: she was frightened. But sacrificing her ease for someone else made her feel alive.

She was taken aback by Conrad's face, which was covered in bruises and sticking plaster. His eyes were almost shut. Though he smelt of aftershave, he did not look in any condition to use a razor, except maybe an electric one. He had donned a safari suit and a cravat. She wore the businesslike clothes in which she had met Michael Chan that morning. Rather than go on being dishonest to Tom, which she would have had to do if she went home, she had filled the hours before dinner at a cinema.

The interior of the flat was not so ugly as she had expected. Mrs Smith must have restrained him. At one end of the living-room, a table with candles on it was laid for dinner. At the other, both the armchairs had objects preventing anyone from sitting on them. Instead of sharing the sofa with him, as he must have intended, she removed a pile of magazines from one of the chairs. He asked her what she would have to drink.

'Mineral water, please.'

He wanted her to have something stronger, but she was adamant. She was here to impose her will. Although she could not see what he was doing as he poured, she was fairly sure he had no chance to adulterate the water. It tasted fine.

Conrad sat down on the sofa. 'I'm nobody's fool,' he said. 'I wouldn't have been able to set up in the cut-throat world of English interior design if I was. So I've a shrewd idea that you've come here to do a deal. I say we cut the small talk and reach terms.'

'Very well,' she said, not that she liked agreeing to anything proposed by him. 'We'll start with your side of the bargain. You go to the police and tell them you're withdrawing your statement and don't want them to prosecute, as you realize you provoked Major Cheney. How much you'll have to do to get them to drop the case, I don't know, but I won't be satisfied until they have.'

'It wouldn't be easy to go back on my evidence to the police. They could accuse me of wasting their time.'

He looked at her out of his puffy eyes. She turned away, resolved to keep silent. His conceit was infinite. He seemed to think he was making a good impression on her.

Conrad stared at her profile. There was really no choice, not that he needed to tell her that. He had never seen a woman so attractive. The idea that he had her in his power almost made him faint.

'But I really like a girl who knows her own mind,' he said. 'I think I can fulfil my side of the deal, provided I can count on you to fulfil yours.'

'Of course I will,' she said. 'How could you doubt it?'

'I'm prepared to let bygones be bygones,' he said, 'but I thought your behaviour yesterday wasn't all that promising.'

'You mean you thought I would be determined to bring a prosecution?'

'Oh no. You wouldn't have stood a chance.' He laughed at her fancy. 'But the other thing. Well, for a time you gave me the impression you weren't too keen on me. Not that you'll be disappointed, I assure you. In fact, I defy a younger man to match me. You'll find that the mature man has everything going for him, and in my case under uniquely reassuring conditions for the woman.'

'You can't mean this, Conrad.'

'Wait and see. You may imagine you'll spring your friend from gaol just by spending a night with me, but what I'm telling you is that you'll want more. I have an unusual approach which I think will appeal to you.' She'd heard that line when he was selling a lurid colour scheme to some Japanese. They refused it.

She wondered which was the safest way for her to dis-illusion him. To bring the whole bogus edifice of his pride crashing down might make him uncontrollable.

'One difficulty remains to be resolved,' he said. 'The order of events. Do I go to the police before we two get together, or after?'

'Before,' she said.

'But I don't know whether I can trust you.'

'You should be pleased I haven't been to the police myself. I could sue you for actual bodily harm committed yesterday morning at the gallery.'

'Your word against mine. Anyhow, I didn't leave a mark on you.'

She took one of the photographs from her bag, stepped forward, put it on the coffee table, which stood between them, and retreated to her chair. He advanced, collected it and, to her relief, went back to the sofa. Here he pored over the picture as though it were a piece of pornography.

'My first present from you,' he said. 'I shall treasure it.'

'Please, Conrad, you don't see why I came here. The deal, as you call it, is this. I promise not to sue you provided you drop your case.'

'That's not a fair exchange. My charge is all set up. The

defendant has admitted he did it. Yours hasn't started, and the defendant won't plead guilty. I'd be forced to tell the court that from the way you asked me into that little room, and from the number of men who came to visit you at work, the magistrates should realize you're not as prim and proper as you claim. I wasn't born yesterday, Belinda. I know a highly-sexed woman when I see one.'

'If you're rejecting my offer, I may as well go.'

'I didn't reject your offer. I just said it wasn't fair. You've got to offer more. For a start, you ought to stay to dinner.'

She wondered what to do. He had been as creepy as she expected, but it seemed he might give in. He was more pitiable than menacing.

'I get so tired of eating on my own,' he said. 'I bought the steak for us.'

'I'll only stay to eat.'

'Wait while I cook.'

A little while later, he came back with two cold plates of overdone steak, each garnished with a cold tomato. The meat was tough. He poured her a glass of red wine. It tasted foul, so she left it. As he swigged away at the stuff himself, drinking the bottle but for her glass, she supposed it was not drugged.

For an hour, he talked about the deficiencies of Mrs Smith. She had maltreated him terribly, not even bearing him children. He was glad she was staying in South Africa to nurse her mother.

For a second hour, he complained that nobody had made him welcome in London. His parents in South Africa were poor whites of English extraction. He had risen by dint of his own abilities in the cut-throat world of interior design in Durban, but found that many of the English whites looked down on him as lower-class, while Afrikaners disliked him because he was English. In London, the English regarded him as South African. Indeed, the liberals thought he was an Afrikaner. They rejected him because he would not say he had left the country from moral outrage and told them the situation in Africa was more complicated than they thought. Meanwhile Britain's racists suspected he had run away from an honest bit of Kaffir-bashing. He could see they did not believe his account of his military service.

The usual mixture of boasting, resentment and general nastiness, Belinda thought. Poor man. However many countries he tried to start a new life in, people still would not like him.

'If you'll come and have dinner with me again, I'll drop the case,' he said.

'All right.'

'But I've got to have a guarantee that you'll come. You see this knife?' He had picked up a carving knife, darted round the table and was standing behind her before she realized her danger. The flat of the blade pressed against her throat. She stared at his empty chair. Over it, there was a mirror in which she saw his grotesquely wounded face.

'It doesn't feel nice, does it,' he said. 'I should keep still if I were you.'

A hand slowly made its way over her shoulder. His head had dropped too low for her to see it in the mirror. It must be close to hers. The hand left her shoulder, descended in front of her. Turning her eyes down, she could see it. The knife trembled as Conrad leant forward. She thought of offering to undress herself. Anything would be preferable to that hand pulling at her garments. The hand reached out for her wine glass, picked it up and brought it to her lips.

'I don't like guests who spurn my hospitality,' he said, tipping the glass so that some of the wine ran into her mouth and some over her chin. 'Mind your table manners in future. It wounds your host to be rejected.'

All at once the knife was removed, he had sprinted back round the table and was holding it against his own throat.

'I'm sorry I alarmed you,' he said. 'I wanted you to know how frightening it is. Will you hold the knife against me?'

She shook her head.

'Drink my wine.'

She drank a sip.

'This is how I know you'll come. See me with the knife against my throat. Know my terror. Know I'll die if you don't visit me again after I've been to the police.'

Belinda stood up, walked round the table and quietly removed the knife from him.

'Thank you so much for dinner,' she said, her hand on his shoulder.

'Thank you for coming. Nobody is so kind to me as you,' he said in a self-pitying voice. 'Usually a girl with your looks would avoid me like the plague. You'd think I was going to rape you or something. You'd prefer to choose someone else. Then it isn't called rape, it's called making love. How can I get love without demanding it? You'd never offer it to me. I'm the kind of man you have to be protected against, because I haven't any self-restraint. I'd like you to tie me up. Then I'd feel safe.'

'How do you think I feel, Conrad? If you thought about that, life might get better. You've spent hours telling me how nasty everyone is to you, but what about your behaviour to me? Most people won't come to see you because they're afraid you're going to attack them.'

'I've got yards and yards of rope.'

'Give me a ring when you've dealt with the police,' she said, and left the emotional cripple to fend for himself. She had no intention of seeing him again. Even a girl who had spent years with David Cheney, and then risked her skin to try to save him from gaol, sometimes saw there were limits to what she could do for men.

Fourteen

She walked to Victoria Station from Conrad's flat. Despite the length of his complaints, it was not yet eleven o'clock. Having telephoned Lindy to say she was all right, she caught a District Line train to Hammersmith. Usually she would have brought her car, to avoid walking after dark and using the Underground, which she detested.

Tonight she had to wait eleven minutes for a train, so the number of passengers was considerable. She got a seat, but in a carriage harangued by a drunk. She wished she had taken a taxi, and knew if she had she would have accused herself of extravagance.

Having tried to rescue David, she was thrown back on the intractability of her own problems. She must have a long talk with Tom. He would, she was sure, have argued that her sense of obligation towards David was exactly the sort of bond with the past she should sever; have tried to stop her from going to see Conrad. But now she had been, she needed to tell him what had happened, and especially about the knife. She could assure him tonight that she was ready, in his company and subject to future knife attacks, to make a new beginning. Today he might have had some ideas about what they should do. His commitment to pottery seemed weak.

More than anything, she wanted to spend time with him. Love takes time. The careerists who took her out had too little time for love.

But when she let herself in, she found that Tom was drinking hot chocolate with her mother.

'Mummy! I thought you weren't coming until the Flower Show.'

'Darling heart, I didn't either, but there's been an emergency. Aunt Christina died on Monday but I only heard today and there was no hope of getting to the funeral unless I got to London tonight, so I rang here and of course you were out and I got your new lodger, and I must say he's made me most welcome.' Mrs Gould beamed at Tom. 'What's more, we've made a plan. Tom says he has no idea whether you're doing anything tomorrow night, but we hope not, because if you aren't, we've got this scheme.'

Belinda sat down. 'As far as I remember, I'm not doing anything,' she said.

'Oh good.' Her mother gave ludicrous emphasis to the word 'good'. 'Because, you see, Hamish Stuart rang, wanting you, and I hadn't seen him since his engagement was announced, though I did write, and so I said I would simply love to meet Ann-Louise if there was a chance while I was in London, but I supposed it was much too short notice to suggest tomorrow night, as on Friday I simply must return to your dear papa. Since you do usually sweetly have a tiny weeny drinks party for me when I'm here, I took my courage in both hands and asked Hamish would there be any chance of their coming then. And as luck would have it they can! I said of course we'd have to cancel if you'd already arranged something, but otherwise we'd expect them about seven. You don't mind, do you? We needn't have anyone else, though I did ask Tom, who I may say has waited on me hand and foot, if he would like to invite Clarissa. He's going to ring her in the morning. We've had such a lovely chat! I do think you've struck lucky in your new lodger.'

'You two seem to have arranged everything,' Belinda said. 'I hope Clarissa can come. I'd like to meet her.'

'Tom says we mustn't be over-optimistic. The hours hospital doctors have to work are a disgrace.'

'I'm sorry to hear about Aunt Christina.'

'The plucky old bird was over ninety. I felt I must go to the funeral for Edith's sake. It's at noon. Tom checked the trains to Winchester.'

'Did you get the job?' he asked.

'Oh yes!' her mother shrieked. 'I quite forgot the job. Tom told me the appalling saga about the brute at the gallery. What happened tonight?'

'Lindy doesn't know.'

'I say, you've spilt something on your blouse, you silly girl. You should put it in to soak.'

'Yes, Mummy.' How did she manage when Mummy wasn't there?

'Still, we mustn't sit up half the night talking. Tom probably wants to get to sleep.'

'My pampered lodger could go to his room.'

'I know. It's too awful. He insists I sleep in it. By the time I got here he'd cleared out all his things and put clean sheets on the bed. I warned him that though you were told when you bought this sofa it made a comfortable bed, I couldn't with the best will in the world say I'd ever had a sound night's sleep on it. But he wouldn't take no for an answer.'

'I can sleep anywhere,' Tom said, 'so please don't hurry on my account. You and Belinda probably have lots of family things to talk about. I can go next door and read a book.'

'You'll make someone a good husband,' Mrs Gould said.

Belinda persuaded her mother to go and have a bath. The moment she and Tom were left alone, he caught her in his arms. She struggled in silence to escape.

'Nobody's ever pampered me like you,' he whispered, holding her fast.

'Stop it,' she hissed. She would rather die than be found embracing him.

'Pamper me first.'

To get rid of him, she submitted to a kiss. His behaviour

118

was beyond the pale. At any instant, her mother might come back.

'I'll show you how the sofa unfolds,' she said, extricating herself. They were at opposite ends of it when her mother did return, to ask which towel she should use. Belinda went to find one for her, and collect bedding for Tom.

He watched her arrange it. 'It sounds as if your mother's in the bath,' he said.

'I've been attacked enough for one evening,' she warned him, though he was sitting quietly. She told him about Conrad and the knife. 'I know I'm going to have nightmares about the hand reaching down in front of me. I couldn't tell where it was going. That was the worst, not knowing where his horrid, stubby fingers would go. I nearly forgot about the knife.'

'I'd like to comfort you,' he said, and kept a safe distance.

His caution roused the opposite reaction to his earlier audacity. She began to feel daring herself.

'Well, why don't you?' she asked, her heart thumping within her.

A distant splosh, as of a hippopotamus getting out of a river, told them her mother's bath was over.

'Too risky,' he said, picking up a book.

Her frustration was intense. She wanted to throw something at him. Every one of her love affairs must be doomed. She remembered a dinner when she was twenty-two or -three. A shy man, ten years older than herself, had taken her out. They went to a restaurant where they were given a corner table, sitting on a banquette with their backs to the wall. He had told her on an earlier occasion that he loved her, but feared, by pressing her for an answer, he would be a nuisance to her. Tonight he made a successful effort to be amusing without being pushy.

Towards the end of dinner, he smiled at something.

'What?' she asked.

'I'm sorry, I was laughing at myself. It must be irritating.'

She forced him to explain.

119

'I was laughing at myself because I wanted to put my arm round you.'

'Well, why don't you?'

He did so; called for the bill. Outside the restaurant, in the dark of the street, they kissed, and walked with their arms round each other; found a cab; went to his flat.

When they were inside, and he put his arms round her again, and she rested hers on him, she said: 'I love you in context.' The daring of the restaurant had vanished. She feared she had been too bold. He was so sincere that as soon as she suspected there were limits to her feelings for him, she had to say so.

He gave a laugh. 'You sound like someone who read English,' he said (which she had done, at Exeter University). She remembered his eyes were kind. She could not remember his name. It went no further: he found, despite his good intentions, that he could not exist without an answer. After prevaricating a little, she told him she did not love him. She was not sure if she did, but he craved certainty. Had he given her time, she might have loved him, except he made her into too much of a princess.

Tom avoided that error. He did not deign to look up from his book. Almost choking, she left the room. She asked her mother if she had everything she needed, said good night to her, used the bathroom, went to her own room and prepared herself for bed. The loneliness of her bed, the large bed of the modern girl who keeps her options open, had started to repel her. She wanted someone there with whom she could share the most normal things; not for delirious sex sessions but for company.

Her face was wet. She felt in the darkness for a handkerchief. She was angry with Tom, the way he took advantage of her, his ingratiating manner with her mother, his mockery of both of them, his lies – it would be foolish to think Clarissa anything but a lie. How could she, Belinda, who in Mrs Stuart's words had 'always been steady', have lowered her guard to let him in? He must go. While he stayed, however, he might treat her with elementary consideration. 'I'd like to comfort you,' he had said, and sat in his chair reading a book.

Some time later, she heard him go into the bathroom – the cord you pulled to turn on the light made an audible click – and after a minute or two leave again, and without thinking of her go back to the living-room. The passage light, shining under her door, went out. She was alone. If her mother hadn't been next door, she would have gone along the passage and shouted at him. He was a pig, but despite the strength of her feeling against him she fell asleep.

It was pitch black when she awoke. She was almost certain someone else was in the room; remembered she had left the window open a crack; wanted to cry out. For a few moments, the silence was so complete she thought she must be mistaken. Then a board creaked and she felt a faint tug on the duvet. Someone lifted it to get in beside her. The person moved with agonizing slowness. It must be Tom, yet she did not believe it was. A hand found her hair, crept to her mouth, held it shut. She leapt at the sudden pressure, jerking her head away, unable to tell whose urgent 'ssh' it was. The spasm of her limbs and bedclothes subsided and she heard Tom whispering:

'Careful, you almost kneed me in the balls.'

'Go back to bed,' she breathed, finding his shoulder with her arm and drawing him against her.

'Mummy's fast asleep. I could hear her breathing.'

'Ssh. She's a very light sleeper. Please go back.' Her clinging arms belied her. Enduring his cold feet, a toenail which scratched her leg and the fear of discovery, she held him and settled once more to sleep.

His arm, on which her full weight seemed to press, started to go numb. He eased his position. The top of her head was under his chin. As he found his way to her mouth, he had no help from her. She gave him a drowsy kiss and tried to curl up again.

When he persisted, she turned her back. He was like one

of her sister Charlotte's children, climbing into her bed determined to play. That is why men and women like being in love. It gives them the chance to act like children; to play, fight, weep.

Belinda did not want to play. She wanted to sleep in his arms. He pulled so hard on one of her knees that she had to roll over on her back. Dumb and blind he started to explore her, a body over which he had not yet ventured by touch and smell alone, to kiss and stroke her with abandon, every part of her and not quietly. If only he would hurry up. On this of all nights, he seemed to want to hang back until he was certain she was ready. He went on and on caressing her. Could he not tell she was ready? He had started this. He ought to end it. She found her handkerchief and pushed it into her mouth, pulled his head to hers, felt him enter her and with frenzied strokes finish.

They must have made a terrible racket. The handkerchief did not work as well as she had expected.

Fifteen

'He took her up in a hot-air balloon and proposed marriage to her,' Ann-Louise said on Thursday morning while she brewed coffee.

Given time to think, Hamish could have listed several reasons why his fiancée should not have said this. He disliked talking at breakfast on weekdays. Besides, Ann-Louise might happen to have an easy day ahead, but he should have left for work an hour ago. His insurance firm let him take time off for politics but expected him to make it up at the start and end of the day. It was because of the City's Big Bang, which so far as he could see meant you had to miss breakfast, lunch and even dinner. Mealtimes were spent at your desk, competing with your colleagues to show commitment. As for such traditional diversions as a round of golf on the afternoons not devoted to finishing lunch, he supposed that would now be a sacking offence, though it had been commonplace among senior members of the firm when he started there.

Moreover, since he was behind schedule, the post had come before he left, and it contained some stuff from the candidates' department at Conservative Central Office. He was quickly trying to understand what it meant.

'Oh really?' he replied. God knows who she was talking about.

'And she refused him! He thought he could sweep her

off her feet, especially as he'd taken her to France before going up in the balloon. But what she told me was that being stuck together in that basket made her realize how it would feel being married to him. Are you listening, Hamster?'

'Haven't missed a word.'

'All right. What did I say?'

'It struck me how sensible I was not to take you up in a balloon when I proposed,' Hamish said, his nose still buried in correspondence. 'That bistro was just the ticket.'

'I would still like to go in one, though. Here's some coffee.'

'Thanks. You couldn't be a darling and answer the phone, could you?'

'Yes, my liege. Your wish is my command.' She went next door. 'Hamish Stuart's secretary,' she said.

'This is Victor Coleman's office,' a woman replied. 'Is it possible for him to speak to Mr Stuart?'

'I'll see if he's available.' She came back into the kitchen. 'Someone called Victor Coleman for you.'

Hamish leapt up wearing his 'man of destiny' look, as she called it.

'Stop,' she said. 'There is a procedure to be followed. Either I should say "I'm sorry, he's in a meeting, can I take a message?" or I should get the other man on the line first.'

'Give it to me.'

But she took the receiver herself and said: 'Hello, this is Mr Stuart's office. I'm just transferring you.' Then she pressed down on the telephone.

'You idiot,' he said. 'You'll cut him off.'

'No I won't. You hold the receiver and then I'll take my hand off and they'll think I've transferred the call.'

'Hamish Stuart speaking,' he said. What gravitas, Ann-Louise thought. What wisdom beyond even Hamster's years.

'I have Mr Coleman for you,' the secretary at the other end of the line said.

'Hello?' Hamish hazarded.

'Victor Coleman here. I'm afraid I've got bad news.'

'Not Cedric?'

'Massive heart attack last night, on his way back from the toilet, poor bugger. They shouldn't have let him walk in his condition. This morning I got his letter about you. Voice from the grave sort of thing. He says you're just the man for us. Are you a worker? We'll want a worker to hold this seat. A bloody miracle worker.'

'I can't promise miracles but I do promise to work all the hours God made if I am selected as candidate.' Oh Hamster, you sound like a boring backbencher already.

'Then I'd like to meet you. What are you doing tonight?'

'I've got to see some people in Hammersmith at seven. After that I'll be free.'

'Tell you what, I'll pick you up and we'll go and have something to eat. Your missus free?'

'I'm engaged to be married, actually. Yes, she should be free, but isn't it the wrong side of London for you?'

'Suits me fine. I've got to look at a site a bit further out. Just tell me where and I'll pick you up on my way back in, round about eight.'

'Who was that?' Ann-Louise asked when the call was over.

'You remember the chap called Victor who Cedric was going to mention me to? Well, he's asked us out to dinner tonight. Poor old Cedric died, incidentally. I said he would.'

'You also said you wouldn't fight the seat at a by-election.'

'That may well be so, but there's no harm having dinner with Victor. He sounded rather an amusing cove.'

'An amusing cove who wants you to work every hour God made? What about me?'

'Darling Antelope, you know you always come first. It's just that I've a sort of sixth sense that Central Office could put some pressure on me to fight this seat, so I ought to take an interest. If you've time, you might like to change into something a bit dressier for tonight. Victor may take us somewhere rather grand.'

Mrs Gould suffered from train fever: Belinda had agreed to have breakfast so early that her mother would have an hour and a half to get to Waterloo Station, in order to catch the train before the one she needed. As a result, Belinda had to set her alarm clock earlier still. She sent Tom tiptoeing along the passage, had a quick bath and took her mother a cup of tea.

'I must say I slept like an absolute top,' Mrs Stuart said at breakfast, with evident truthfulness. 'I'm afraid you're looking the worse for wear, Tom. Those sofa-beds are a scandal.'

'Belinda's the one who's yawning. There's nothing wrong with your bed, is there?'

'I had a dream about a performing flea,' she said.

'After that rumpus at the gallery you're bound to feel unsettled until you get another job,' Mrs Gould said. She needed to believe that barring temporary setbacks, her daughter was all right. 'At least you've got a lodger,' she added brightly. 'You know, since I'm ready I think I'll go.'

'What do you mean, performing flea?' he asked angrily when they were alone.

'Darling, it was only my warped sense of humour.' She smoothed his hair and sat down beside him.

'Many a true word spoken in jest,' he said, frowning as he would when he wanted her full attention.

'It was wonderful for me, really it was. Otherwise I wouldn't have dared tease you. I so wanted to be with you last night.'

'Great welcome you gave me.'

'That's because I was embarrassed. I was hoping we'd just sleep in each other's arms.'

'So you didn't like all the trouble I took.'

'Surely you could tell how much I liked it?'

'I see. You think I'm inexperienced.'

'I couldn't care less how experienced you are. It really doesn't matter compared to what we feel for each other. You remember when you said you loved me? That's what matters.'

He knew she wanted him to repeat the words. She had brought their talk from a squabble to a moment of truth, or falsehood.

'I love you Tom,' she said. 'I don't know why. Men seem to think women have a checklist of things they want. When you came to dinner here, you told me I wanted an old rectory. Now you're telling me I want orgasms. I'm sure I want these things, especially if you tell me so. But they've nothing to do with love. Love is personal.'

He gazed at her. If she thought women weren't attracted by power, money and looks she was off her head.

'How can I explain?' she mused. 'Suppose some guests go to a wedding and apart from wondering whether the marriage will last, they try to work out who's doing best from it. She's better connected, he's richer, she's more attractive but her health's bad, he's never had a serious illness but he's been married before, on the other hand she's a flirt. So is it a fair exchange or has one of them scored off the other? To judge by her mother's expression, she thinks her daughter's sold herself cheap. The dresses on the bride's side of the church are unfashionable, but at least her menfolk's morning coats are gentlemanly garments, inherited from their fathers, not hired, like those of the groom's supporters, at Moss Bros.

'If the bride and groom think in the same way about each other, they're not in love.'

'They're bound to notice,' he said.

'Even if they do, they should put all that social thing in its place. It's trivial compared to love.'

'Your attitude's fine if you can maintain it during a lifetime in a hovel. If I married you, I'd want to give you a proper house.'

'An old rectory? Thanks very much, but I wouldn't judge your love for me by the standard of the house you provided. I wouldn't judge you at all. Can't you see that? I'm not a calculating machine, working out how you measure up to some standard of masculine perfection.'

'You're making excuses for me.'

'No.'

'All right. For yourself. How can you justify having an affair with a twenty-four-year-old layabout who hasn't got a job? You need some fairly advanced ideals to cope with that.'

She feared that by posing as the upholder, on her behalf, of prudence, almost of the arranged marriage, he was trying to wriggle out of his obligation to her. 'I'm too young and feckless for you' was easier to say than 'I don't love you'. She would not ask him to say, as he had said once before, that he loved her. Her pride prevented it, and the words were worthless if he did not say them of his own accord. She started to clear up the breakfast things.

'William contacted me from the pottery yesterday,' he said, trying to ignore her need for tenderness. 'There's a crisis about our studio. I said I'd go and see him this morning.'

'Off you go then.'

He went up to her in the kitchen. Turning to face him, she looked older but no less beautiful. She dazzled him. Her beauty shining through the vulnerability of tiredness and strain seemed to attract him more powerfully than if she had been at the pinnacle of youth. When she was fifty, adolescent boys would wonder if there was something wrong with them because they fancied her more than young women. He felt drunk. He could not imagine how he had been tempted to make this woman suffer, even to derive a thrill from his power to do so. He wanted to make his present feeling for her last for ever. Let him seize the moment of exalted love, a feeling of abandon to his own best instincts beyond anything he had ever known. The idea welling up inside him was so deliciously unusual, it was a masterstroke of daring, a sudden insight of the kind great scientists had, long before they could show why they were right. He was a great general, too. It was as if by a forced march he had moved his whole army so that it appeared at sunrise in the quarter she least expected. He loved to ambush people. This would be the most brilliant ambush of his life, the moment when he prolonged for ever the joy of being with her, possessing her, loving her.

'Will you marry me?' he said.

'What?'

'I want you to marry me.'

'How long have you wanted this?'

'About half a minute.'

'It's the sweetest thing anyone's ever said to me.'

'I didn't say it to be sweet. What's your answer?'

'Give me time.'

'I made a good impression on your mother.'

'I still don't understand how you did that.'

'I showed her a story in the business news about my father's company. It seemed to make up for my lack of breeding.'

'Oh!'

'Answer me.'

'I must have time. My mind can't work as quickly as yours. You've taken me by surprise.'

'I took myself by surprise too.'

She warned herself that he had yielded to an exultant moment. He was like a novice drinker given a new spirit. The first sip tasted so good that he wanted to spend his life gulping it, unaware how it would pall. He thought, in his naïvety, that if he had a limitless supply of Belinda he would be happy. He wasn't in love with her but with the self-indulgent gesture. He was a gambler. He had no

129

judgement, no foresight, no proper fear of wrecking other people's lives. She loved him.

'You go to the pottery and I'll try to think,' she said.

Sixteen

The flowers arrived at Belinda's flat just after five o'clock. A florist had telephoned to check that someone would be there to receive them, but did not reveal the size of the delivery. It looked as though the contents of a shop selling nothing but lilies had been dispatched. Profuse green foliage set off the opulent simplicity of the flowers, which were pure white with a stain of plum pink running down the middle of each petal. The smallest stems were two feet high. She ran out of vases and had to borrow from the firm.

'Isn't there a card?' she asked the man in charge.

'No message, Miss. Where would you like these?'

'Leave them in the corridor, please. You must have some idea?'

'If you want my advice, Miss, it's someone who's fond of you.'

She had never received such a quantity of flowers. She wished lilies weren't associated with death.

Her mother returned just as the men left. Aunt Christina's funeral would usually have been described at length, but tonight Belinda heard nothing of it.

'Don't be ridiculous,' Mummy said. 'You must know who sent them, and whoever it is, you must ask him to the party. If I get cracking, I'll have the ones in your drawing-room sorted by seven.' Mrs Gould loved arranging flowers.

'Haven't you a better pair of scissors? Now give me somewhere to put the bits. That's right. If you don't want to tell
your own mother who sent them, why not telephone him?
Is Clarissa coming?'

'She can't, I'm afraid.'

'So we're reduced to Ann-Louise, Hamish and Tom, plus
you and me, that makes five. What a waste. With flowers
like these you ought to have a proper party.'

'There wouldn't be room.'

'We could manage more than five. Now these, I think,
would look best on the hearth. We aren't going to want a
fire, are we? I haven't seen those nice Scott-Woodhouses
for donkey's years.'

'I had them to dinner last week.' The bell rang: she looked
out of the window. 'Tom must have forgotten his key,' she
said, and went downstairs.

'Is your mother back?' he asked, jumping through the
door and kissing her.

'Unfortunately yes.'

'I guessed she would be. Being a man of infinite tact, I
thought I'd give you these down here.' He took a bunch of
daffodils from behind his back. They were wrapped in the
mauve paper used by the late-night shop on the corner, and
were past their best. 'Tell her you asked me to get them for
the party,' he said.

'Thank you very much.'

'Come on, or Mummy will think the lodger's making a
pass.'

He did not ask her whether she had an answer to his
proposal – not that she did – but bounded ahead of her up
the stairs. Just inside the flat, he stopped dead, before
walking slowly into the living-room.

'You may well wonder,' Mrs Gould said. 'It's not every
girl who would be sent flowers like this.'

'But who?'

'She won't say.'

He turned back into the corridor, where Belinda was

scrumpling up the piece of mauve paper. His daffodils shared a bucket with some lilies.

'Who sent you this lot?' he asked.

'I don't know. They've only just come.'

'May as well get rid of mine.' He stooped and before she could stop him, plucked them out of the water.

'Give them back.'

'Mrs Gould,' he called. 'Amid this cornucopia, I have identified a substandard bunch. Look.'

'Oh yes, frightful. I can't imagine how those got muddled up. Throw them away this instant.' She nodded at the black plastic sack which she was using for unwanted pieces of stalk and leaf.

When her mother's back was turned, Belinda retrieved the overblown daffodils, found a large jam jar and went to put them in her bedroom. Tom had been co-opted to help with the arranging. She shut the door and picked up the telephone by her bed.

'Michael Chan, please. It's Belinda Gould.'

'Belinda,' he said when he came on the line. 'Many congratulations. I really didn't think you stood much of a chance. I hope you didn't have too unpleasant a time with Smith?'

'How did David find out it was me?'

'Because at first the police wouldn't accept that Smith just wanted to withdraw his statement, so he told them you were going to bring a case against him unless he dropped his own, which, though they hadn't heard from you, squared with Major Cheney's evidence. After a bit they seem to have lost sympathy with Smith, and concluded that to bring a case on his behalf was more than their time was worth. I may say I only discovered this because I made a routine call to see how things were going. Then I had to pass on the police explanation to Major Cheney, whom they still want to caution.'

'But his career will be all right?'

'Between ourselves, I understand that his commanding

officer had refused his resignation, telling him to come back in a week's time. It is all a triumph for the informal British way of doing things. If I can ever be of help to you, please give me a ring.'

She sat on her bed wondering what to do. She did not want to leave David unthanked, but to ask him here was impossible – except that for the duration of her mother's visit, Tom was her lodger. But Tom would go mad if she asked him. She didn't like the thought of David sitting alone on his night of deliverance, telling himself that he never expected to hear from her, since he was thanking her, not vice versa. On the other hand, it was silly of him to embarrass her by turning her flat into a florist's, instead of sending one good bunch. He could not even get flowers in proportion. She did not see how desperate he was becoming.

She went back to the living-room.

'Well?' her mother said. 'Did your call uncover the truth?' She and Tom had heard the other telephone chink.

'It wasn't a call to whoever sent the flowers,' she said.

Faced with such stubborn resistance, Mrs Gould called on her ally. 'Tom, you're a man. How would you feel if you sent some flowers to a girl and she didn't even ring you up to say thank you?'

'I've never sent flowers like these.'

'Exactly. Think what these must have cost!' Mrs Gould attempted to compute the price of the flowers, which could not, she reckoned, have cost less than a fiver each. The poorer she got, the less she could contain herself. 'In short, whoever sent these needs a wife to stop him being so extravagant. But how are we ever going to get my daughter married if she won't ring to say thank you?'

'You're as bad as Mrs Stuart,' Belinda said.

'At least she has some effect on her son. I appeal to you, Tom. Tell Belinda she should at least ask whoever sent the flowers to her party, so he can see how nice they look.'

'No gentleman would expect a woman to do that,' Belinda

intervened. 'The thought of making her a gift in order to put her under an obligation would appal him.'

'That's out of date,' Tom said.

'On the contrary, my mother taught me that whatever else changes, the difference between gentlemen and the rest is eternal.'

'If he's a gentleman, how much more reason to invite him,' Tom argued. 'We can be sure his behaviour will be immaculate.'

'David Cheney sent the flowers,' Belinda said. 'He always gave me lilies.'

'I'd love to meet him. You know, Mrs Gould, he's so perfect that when he found Conrad had maltreated Belinda, he beat him up. The police wanted to charge him with assault but Belinda got him off the hook. It's a moving story. I myself feel, as heir to new money, that I could learn from talking to a man whose money is slightly older, albeit diminished by indiscriminate expenditure on flowers.'

'I'll go and ring him.' She wasn't going to yield to his sarcasms.

'Thank you for the lovely flowers,' she began.

'They're nothing to what you've done for me. I'm afraid they must be a nuisance. I'll tell the people to take them away again if you like.'

'My mother's here. She's helping to arrange them. In fact, she's taken over completely.'

'Oh good.'

'And we're having one or two people to drinks this evening. I thought you might like to come, if you're free.'

'Are you sure?'

'To see the flowers, I mean.'

'As a friend.'

'Yes, as a friend. Apart from my mother, the other people will be Hamish, Ann-Louise and my new lodger, who's called Tom Coleman.'

'All right. Thank you. I won't stay long: I'm invited to

some wretched dinner.' She knew he wanted her to ask if he could get out of dinner.

'Tell me more about Clarissa,' Ann-Louise was saying. She, Mrs Gould and Tom formed one group; Hamish, David and Belinda another.

'She's hard to describe.'

'Do try,' Mrs Gould said. 'What colour hair does she have?'

'Much the same as Ann-Louise's. In fact, she's similar to Ann-Louise in a number of ways. You know, looks her best in fluorescent green' – 'a short skirt of this colour was, to Hamish's discomfiture, his fiancée's idea of something dressier – 'and atrociously left-wing.'

'I'm dining tonight with a pillar of the Conservative Party,' she retorted.

'Who's that?' Mrs Gould asked.

'Now I come to think of it, he's probably related to Tom. He's called Victor Coleman.'

'But you're quite right!' Mrs Gould exclaimed. 'What a coincidence! He's Tom's father. There was a bit in yesterday's paper about him. Belinda, where's yesterday's paper?'

'I don't believe you,' Tom said to Ann-Louise, while Mrs Gould went to look for the article.

'Treasurer in Cedric Williams' seat. Cedric dies. Hamish Stuart groomed to carry the can for losing the by-election.'

'Where are you meeting him?'

'He's picking us up here. I'm needed to prove that Hamish is heterosexual.'

'I expect my father will bring proof of his own.'

'But you haven't, Tom. Not unless you can produce Clarissa.'

'I said you'd pass for her.'

'Would I?'

'I hope so.'

'Here's the article,' Mrs Gould said. 'It's about trends in

the property market. Let's see. "Victor Coleman, Chairman of Coleman Country Homes, the Essex-based developer, which last week reported a 12.4 per cent rise in annual pre-tax profits to £17.25 million, said that even with mortgage rates at their present level . . . "'

'Yes, yes,' Tom said. 'It's not all that interesting. It's about money.'

'May I?' Hamish asked, and took the paper to one corner. This brought Belinda and David into the other group. She was relieved to find him behaving so well. His main concern, once he had praised the arrangement of the flowers, was to stop people talking about them.

'What is it that you do for your father, Tom?' Mrs Gould asked. She could not tell what proportion of the company was owned by the family, but £17.25 million was so stupendous a sum that they must be rich. They'd made £17.25 million in a single year.

'My most recent service was to tell him about a disused factory where some artists have rented studios. He went to see it this afternoon. His intention is to fill the site with Coleman Country Homes.'

'Would I be right to infer,' David asked, 'that your sympathies are with the artists?'

'He's one of them!' Ann-Louise said. 'He's a potter.'

'Oh yes,' David said. 'I believe you've been mentioned to me.'

Everyone except Mrs Gould felt it had been a mistake to say Tom was a potter.

'Doesn't Clarissa want you to give up the pottery and start working for your father?' Ann-Louise asked, trying to retrieve the situation. 'Clarissa is Tom's girlfriend,' she explained to David.

'It's true she's not very keen on pottery, and since I'm mad about her, I suppose I'll have to give in.'

'Property must pay better than pottery,' Mrs Gould said.

'Didn't I hear that you're developing a table-lamp?' David asked. He could not stop himself.

'No, no. Whoever told you that is an idiot. I must hurry or I'll be late for Clarissa.'

'Odd that he didn't stay to see his father,' Mrs Gould said.

'Mummy, he had no idea his father was coming tonight. Obviously he'd already planned to meet his friend.'

'Well, I do think we should have the father in for a drink,' declared Mrs Gould. 'He sounds a very interesting man.'

'I assure you there's no need,' Hamish said. 'When the bell goes, Ann-Louise and I will slip away.'

But when the bell sounded, a few minutes later, it was Belinda who ran downstairs. She wanted to see this man whose son would hardly talk about him.

Victor Coleman looked too young and energetic to be Tom's father. At first sight, she would have taken him for an elder brother.

'Victor Coleman,' he said. 'I've come for Hamish Stuart. Are you his girl?'

'No,' she laughed. 'I'll go and tell them you're here. Do come up for a drink if you'd like to.'

'Pity we can't put you on our leaflets,' he said, following her.

'Hamish, this is Mr Coleman.'

'Pleased to meet you,' Victor said.

'And this is Ann-Louise, his fiancée, and my mother, Letty Gould, and David Cheney.'

'And what's your name?' Victor asked, when he had done the round.

'Belinda.'

'Well, Belinda, I can see you're fond of flowers.' Everyone was amused.

'Mr Coleman,' Mrs Gould began, 'you will never believe the most amazing coincidence which I have discovered – all because I was reading about your company in yesterday's business news.'

'What's that, Letty?' he asked, accepting a gin and tonic from Belinda.

138

'Your son Tom is my daughter's lodger!'

'Poor girl.'

'I must say he's a really charming young man. He helped me arrange the flowers.'

'That sounds like him. Did he tell you about his invention?'

'His invention? He didn't say a word about it.'

'My son has invented a table-lamp. At least he says he has. This afternoon I called to have a look at his studio. I asked him to show me this lamp with which he is going to make his fortune. He pointed at a sort of flower-pot. Even as a flower-pot it wouldn't work. It had holes in it. "Where does it turn on?" I asked him. "Oh well," he said. "I haven't done the electrics yet." "In any case," I said, "the mouth of this pot is too wide. The light fitting will fall in." "You're right," he said. "It'll need a special design." "How long will that take?" I asked. He's had getting on for a year. "It's not always a good idea to hurry experimental work," he said. What I'd like to know is who he lives off while he's experimenting.'

'Good question,' David said.

'The cost of living these days is astronomical,' Mrs Gould agreed.

'For too long we in this country have failed to realize that there is no such thing as a free lunch,' Hamish asserted.

'Yes there is,' Ann-Louise said.

'Darling, it's been proved beyond the shadow of a doubt that there isn't.'

'I can see that someone has to pay for the lunch,' Belinda said, 'but surely it is possible to give it to someone else?'

'Free handouts have ruined this country,' Victor said. 'The idea that you can get something for nothing. I don't think the government should rescue people from their own stupidity. Nor should parents.'

'We'd have liked to give Belinda help with buying a house, but it's so expensive, isn't it,' Mrs Gould said; fell into confusion when she remembered she was talking to a builder who had made £17.25 million last year.

'I do think we are going to have to have further major reforms of the welfare state to ensure that help is accurately targeted at those who really need it,' Hamish said.

'We used to manage perfectly well without a welfare state,' David declared.

'Oliver Twist yielded to pure greed when he asked for more?' Belinda asked.

'I have never found Dickens's novels either believable or readable,' David said.

'With great respect, Belinda, we are not now trying to cope with the troubles to which Dickens drew attention, namely the consequences of the 1832 Poor Law,' Hamish said, feeling rather pleased with himself for this specialist bit of information. He could not remember whether it was 1832 or 1834, but what matter? 'Oliver Twist and his friends have long since been given more. Too much more.'

'As you can see any night when you leave the theatre and the Strand is full of people sleeping in cardboard boxes,' Ann-Louise said. 'It makes my blood boil to find boys and girls living so well.'

'It makes my blood boil when my company offers the chance to any able-bodied lad to learn a trade and we still can't get enough people,' Victor said.

'It's the same in the army,' David agreed. 'If they want to sleep rough, why don't they come and do it on exercise with us? Then when they want to come out of the army we'll start them off in a trade and they can go and work for Victor.'

'In fact,' Belinda said, 'life is an extraordinarily easy business with benefactors like you two around. Nobody ever has a broken home. Nobody suffers from mental illness. We're all able to look after ourselves and find satisfying, well-paid jobs. Anyone who doesn't is a malingerer. I must be a malingerer.'

'You're unemployed?' Victor said.

'Since Tuesday morning.'

'Give me a ring if the building trade interests you. Thanks for the drink.'

After everyone had gone, her mother kept on saying what a success the drinks party had been, as though repeating this made it true. Belinda recalled the malignant expression on David's face when he found Tom was her lover.

Seventeen

That night David dreamed of Belinda. He was at a party, conducting, as duty prescribed, a lively conversation with someone, but decided that what he wanted was a whisky and soda. So he went into another room and found a smallish wine glass. By the time he had put whisky and ice into it, there was room for virtually no soda. He didn't mind.

The new room was emptier and darker. It might be an open courtyard. He was standing next to Belinda. They were by a fountain, and she looked at him and said nothing, but half turned and went on talking to someone else. She could still see him. Her face had coarsened, her cheeks were swollen and the way she stood was more brazen, but he could overlook that. Chiefly he was astonished that she chose not to address a word to him. He stood alone with his glass, feeling conspicuous, wondering whether he should go back next door and attempt to resume the conversation he had broken off. If she said nothing to him, he could say nothing to her. He could not believe that she would say nothing to him. He did not try to hear what she and her companion, who was in shadow, were saying. They talked in low voices. The fountain trickled water over a rock. He sipped his drink and found it was mostly ice.

On waking, he was surprised his dream had been melancholy rather than desperate. It was worse being awake. However bad separation from her felt, it was worse to see her and have no hope. He wondered what he had done wrong. He ought to have married her first and slept with her afterwards, but that had become a breach of etiquette.

Though the whole relationship had been on her terms, the freedom to leave him had not benefited her. She was acting like a whore who didn't even charge for her services. Any man she liked could exploit her without providing for her. She must be subsidizing Tom Coleman, a youth whose unreliability was obvious to the meanest intelligence. Her choice of Tom made David despair. Tom's own father had revealed his son as a liar, a fraud who claimed to be an artist in order not to work, as if art could be accomplished without discipline. What could attract Belinda to him? The young man had battened on to her like some filthy parasite. David couldn't bear to think of Tom holding her flesh, yet couldn't stop himself thinking about them. It was incredible that she had not yet coarsened, as in the dream.

When Michael Chan reported that Belinda had persuaded Conrad Smith to withdraw his evidence, David's heart leapt within him. She did care after all. He glimpsed the bliss he would have felt if she really loved him. Then she asked him to the party. He saw afterwards that her mother must have put her up to that. He would be all right if he wanted to marry one of those mothers. Instead he made himself late for dinner to be received with chilly kindness by Belinda, see the potter play the part of lodger for Mrs Gould's benefit and be drawn with the others into the deceit.

Hamish didn't like it, of course. Hamish was a decent fellow. But it was clear that Ann-Louise was enjoying every minute. She might even have told him on purpose that here was the potter-boyfriend for whom Conrad had taken David when he visited the gallery. As for the nonsense about Clarissa, it didn't deceive him for a moment.

He was consumed by the selfishness of the miserable. In the last few days, he had heard about a friend whose wife had died of kidney failure at the age of thirty-six, other friends who had lost their first baby, and a sixteen-year-old recruit who had hanged himself at Pirbright, but nobody else's suffering seemed anything compared to his own. The reprieve of his career was worthless if he could not have Belinda.

He saw a girl in a magazine standing in front of a sand dune, her wrists held one in front of the other against her forehead to keep the sun from her eyes. She was advertising a 'light cotton top'; resembled Belinda. The garment, a sort of jersey, fell loosely over her body from neck to waist. Her breasts were revealed by two slight curves, these and the slackness where the cotton dropped away suggesting such beauty of shape, such generosity of delicate flesh, as to make him cry out. He had to do something. He could not spend another four years in the wilderness. Either he must find a true wilderness and kill himself during a journey into it, or he must make a last effort to win her. Passivity was the refuge of inferior minds. He needed a woman, would have taken any woman who chanced to be there, but no woman except Belinda could satisfy his craving not to be deserted.

The first attempt to protect her had been a humiliating failure. She had ended up protecting him. This time he would be more careful.

Tom came back after mother and daughter had retired. Belinda heard him entering the flat. The sofa-bed had been left ready, but as soon as the light in the passage went out, he stepped silently into her room and settled with her. Tonight, to her relief, he did not try to make love. As they drifted to sleep, she felt closer to him than she had ever done. No words came to complicate her love, or provoke unanswerable questions about the future. In the morning, her complacency and his indifference were such that her mother almost found them in each other's arms.

She and Mrs Gould left together, since Belinda, in a fit

of financial terror on Thursday morning, had rung Lindy and arranged a day's temping.

Hamish had a most satisfactory time after the party. Victor's chauffeur drove them in a Bentley to a restaurant in Mayfair. A peroxide blonde was waiting at a table for four. Her clothes were similar to Ann-Louise's, only more risqué. Victor introduced her as Suki, his assistant. Ann-Louise tried to draw her into the conversation, but she did not want to talk. She thought that during dinner, a decorative appearance ended her duties. After a time, Ann-Louise gave up disrupting the conversation which the men had started and pursued thoughts of her own.

Meanwhile Victor told Hamish about the local association, its factions and prejudices, and why, in his opinion, it ought to be possible to hold the seat. There was a good chance that the local Labour Party would choose a weak candidate, not so weak that Walworth Road could stop or remove her, but bad enough to help. The Tories had material about the woman's past that could be used when her selection was secure. There was bound to be a swing against the Government, but the squabbling between the centre parties, and extremism of the Labour candidate, would give dissatisfied Conservatives little choice but to stay loyal or abstain. In his opinion, the Tories would scrape home on a low turnout.

'That may be so,' Hamish said, 'but why should I get the candidacy?'

'What you have to do is act ordinary. Some of the runners will think they're coming down to the sticks to lecture us. We don't want our MP to be some clever Dick, all he's done since leaving college is make tea for ministers, he thinks he's going to be in the Cabinet himself in ten years' time. No more do we want a retread who lost his seat somewhere else and reckons on ignoring us, once we've seen him back in. We want someone we can mould. You've got to be the man who sees things from our point of view, lives among us, knows what it's like to have a mortgage and a season ticket, worries about the standard of behaviour in local schools, realizes it's more important to tell Central Office what we're thinking than tell us what Central Office says is the party line. The man who knows the danger of getting out of touch on issues like crime and immigration. Not that we want you to be disloyal. You do support her, don't you?'

'I think Margaret Thatcher's put the Great back into Great Britain.'

'So do we.'

'I'm one hundred per cent behind the government and would regard it as my duty, if elected, to keep it true to its populist instincts.'

'That's right. Then the selection committee, which is the financial and general purposes committee plus a few co-opted members, would have to decide you were the best compromise candidate to block whichever raving fascist the Young Conservatives put up. I'll be on the committee, so I can tell you how it's going. You've got to spend a lot of time finding out about the constituency. I'll fill you in on local issues like planning.'

'That would be a great help,' Hamish said. He reckoned that Victor was newer to politics than himself, but would be a useful ally.

'Why not put in for the seat yourself?' Ann-Louise asked Victor.

'Can't afford the time. What I want is an MP I can talk to about the things which worry me.' He told Hamish about the short-sightedness of preserving derelict bits of countryside in the Green Belt.

'Did you enjoy your lobster?' Hamish asked Ann-Louise as they were driven home in a car that Victor had insisted on providing.

'It didn't have much flavour,' she said. 'As for our host, he's the sort of man who'll be nice to you as long as you do what he says. He won't tolerate the slightest independence

146

by his son and now he's looking for an MP he can indoctrinate about villages on green-field sites.'

It was no use answering back. Hamish knew he was on to something. He didn't mind a few lectures if he got a seat that would be safe, once the by-election was won. Some of the strongest candidates would decide not to put in for a contest that they expected the Tories to lose. By visiting Cedric, and dining with Victor, he had stolen a march on them. He thought of several other people he would consult.

A few days later, the vice-chairman in charge of candidates rang him to make sure he was going to apply for the seat. The vice-chairman, himself an MP, affected complete certainty that the Tories would hold on to the seat. Any candidate who feared, however, that in the amazing event of a defeat, he might forfeit his chances of finding somewhere else, should be assured that on the contrary, he would win gratitude at the highest level for fighting a good campaign.

'But aren't they rather a bloodthirsty lot?' Hamish asked.

'Strictly in confidence, they are. That's why I'm so anxious that a safe pair of hands like yourself should put in for it. Someone who can handle the press.'

'I've been down there to speak.'

'Oh well, in that case you'll appreciate the very real danger that they'll pick someone unsavoury. We think we can hold it, but only if we find a decent candidate. You did so remarkably well in a tough seat at the general election, bucked the trend and so on, that Number Ten did actually ask if you're in the running. I shouldn't have mentioned that, but it's going to do us a lot of harm if we come unstuck.' It might harm the prospects of the vice-chairman in charge of candidates.

'It would be hopeless to be known as the Central Office candidate,' Hamish said. 'I ought to be the man telling Central Office what they think.'

'My dear chap, you obviously see just what's needed.'

Hamish agreed to put his name forward.

Eighteen

People seldom pay as much attention to us as we fear. For Belinda, her taking of Tom as a lover was a momentous event, but hardly anyone else seemed interested. Her mother, who had plenty to worry about in Yorkshire, thought she had only taken a lodger. David must realize the truth, but had fallen silent again. Hamish was doubtless immersed in politics, while Ann-Louise, apart from her articled clerkship, would be busy organizing the wedding. The pair of them must have gossiped about her liaison, Belinda thought, and left her to it. She would have done the same.

Many others must be aware she had a new boyfriend, but she and Tom got no invitations bearing both their names and he declined to go to parties where she could have taken a partner. She therefore refused all invitations, though he was anxious she should not sacrifice her old friends to him. So long as the two of them were marooned together, she would not mind if her flat were a desert island.

Unlike any man she had lived with before, he was keen on cooking. He would often buy a fish or a piece of meat, and on her return tell her not to worry about supper. But he was slow to start doing anything, and frequently found he lacked some of the ingredients for whatever he decided to make, which meant he had to go to a late-night supermarket to get them.

She forced herself to keep out of the kitchen, to avoid being driven to distraction as he broke, burnt, dented, scratched or otherwise marked her possessions. His cooking was as experimental and impromptu as hers was planned. He was prodigal with olive oil and garlic, and they drank a great amount of wine while waiting to eat, so she was half-drunk by the time they dined.

Afterwards he would never let her wash up, promising to do it tomorrow. He wanted strong coffee, more wine or preferably some kind of spirit, cigarettes, music, sex and talk. Her previous lovers fascinated him. He had favourite stories about them which he asked her to repeat. There were things she would not tell him, as laughter was so liable to be his response.

The former neatness of the flat, indicating a strenuous effort by Belinda to keep up with the housework, gave way to bourgeois-bohemian disorder. He loathed electric light so lit candles when dusk faded into night. She tended to fall asleep after supper, full of food, drink and tiredness. He would draw her sleeping face; wake her with a kiss. He also did a long series of drawings of her washing her hair. She sometimes felt she was being studied by an anthropologist who took no personal interest in her, but treated her as an example of a tribe; even by a zoologist who looked on her as an animal. He wanted to draw her in the bath, said he would have to take the bathroom door off its hinges to make more space.

'You mustn't!' she said, horrified.

'I'm going to do a series of pictures called "The Toilet of Belinda". It'll be the climax of my exhibition. The door has to be removed.'

'No, Tom.'

'What have you got to hide from me?'

'Personal things.'

'Those are what interest me most.'

Some mornings he would try to provoke a reaction by saying, casually, that today he would get rid of that door.

An exhibition of pictures was one of his many fancies. She harboured the same reluctant suspicion about his drawings as his pots: that they showed promise but would not sell. He talked of enrolling at the Slade. Dreams of his own future came and went, sometimes several in the course of a night. He was going to be actor, psychoanalyst, cartoonist, dress designer, restaurateur.

'Where shall we have our restaurant?' he asked.

'Moscow.'

'Yes, and we'll want a farm in the country where the ingredients are grown.'

She looked at the two piles by the sink, one of bleary things that had been washed, or rinsed, the other of things still waiting.

'We'll have a Russian do that,' he said. 'You'll go front of house. I'll be chef.'

'It'll be hard work.'

'I'll get on with planning the menus.'

One day a man rang and left a number with Tom for Belinda to phone.

'A rival,' he said. 'Wouldn't give his name.'

'What shall I do? It's Conrad's flat. He's bound to ring again.'

'He's tried before but wouldn't leave a message. He'd just ask if you were here.'

'Did he mention the knife?'

'If he had, I'd have told him to go ahead. You've waited years for your first suicide.'

'Don't.'

'Let me try the number for you,' Tom said. 'Hello, is that Mr Smith? This is Miss Gould's financial adviser. I understand that you still owe my client arrears of salary, holiday pay and bonus. She has informed me that she will not be contacting you until these outstanding sums have been settled. Goodbye.'

'But I won't be contacting him ever,' she said.

'It doesn't matter. He owes you the money. I think the

least your lodger can do, since I'm not paying rent, is collect bad debts for you.'

'He'll ring me.'

'Bound to.'

'What am I going to do then?'

'Hand him over to me.'

After that, she encouraged Tom to answer the phone. Conrad sent a cheque, which she cleared into her account, and Lindy continued to find well-paid temping for her, so financial disaster was staved off. Tom said he was getting enough money from his mother to buy food and drink. He advised her, during their second bottle of wine one evening, to get a fee-paying lodger to occupy the spare room.

'And see you wandering naked down the passage.'

'That would be one of the attractions.'

'I'd prefer it to be just you and me.'

'We could have three-in-a-bed sex romps.' It was one of the days when he believed in his flair for tabloid journalism.

'Of course, if it was going to be another man, that would be different.'

'What?' Like many who enjoy teasing others, he couldn't take it himself.

'Sorry. I meant a sixteen-year-old nymphette you can bed when you're tired of me.'

'I'll never be tired of you.'

'She'd be under half my age.' Belinda paused. 'When she's the age I am now, I'll be over fifty.'

'But I love you. "Love is not love which alters when it alteration finds." Otherwise I'd never have proposed marriage to you.' It was the first time he had referred to it. For weeks the question had lain with her while she wondered whether he meant what he said, or, to do him justice, whether he would go on meaning it when he stopped desiring her.

'If that's not serious, what is?' he demanded, so fiercely that he betrayed his defensiveness.

He saw she feared to speak her mind because he might

151

not like what she said. She might be going to say they must part. He would show as much regret as he dared.

'If that's not serious, what is?' he prompted.

'Having children.'

Taken off balance, he searched for a reply. 'I thought that would come after getting married,' he said.

'You're very conventional all of a sudden.'

'My father got my mother pregnant with me. I'm why they married.'

'What a lovely reason,' she said, her hold on his arm nearly frantic.

'But the marriage didn't last. She simply couldn't keep up with him as soon as he started being successful.'

'You think I couldn't keep up with you?'

'It's a question of whether you can keep down with me. I've achieved nothing.'

'You will.'

'I've no right to you,' he blurted. 'You ought to marry someone dependable.'

She hid herself in her hands.

'It's what I've said to you before,' he added, trying to bolster his position.

The face which turned to him was so distorted that for a moment he thought she was laughing. 'Why do you always run yourself down?' she cried. 'Can't you accept that I love you? Isn't that enough? Of course it's not enough if you don't love me.' Hysterical sobs prevented her from going on. He was frightened. This suffering was beyond his experience. It was like coming downstairs in the dark, thinking you had reached the last step and falling into unknown depths.

She was in a much worse state than when she came back from Conrad's attack. That was superficial. Tom had entered her heart. She felt as if an iron plate were embedded there, tied by a thin, strong cord to him, and he was pulling it so that she was in agony, and would rather be wrenched apart than go on feeling this, but the plate would not move.

She rested against him, wishing he would make the cord go slack.

'I don't know what came over me,' she said after a long time, though she knew quite well. 'I think I'll have to go to bed.' She felt so tired she might faint. All those nights talking to him, which she had wanted to do. She was happy not sleeping.

'What can I bring you to eat?' he asked. It was nine in the evening, the time it suited him to start preparing supper. They seldom ate before eleven.

She shook her head.

'Have some soup.'

'No.'

'You're cold,' he noticed. 'I'll make you a hot water bottle.' He got her into her nightdress, brought the bottle, put an extra blanket over the duvet until she had warmed up. A little later he came back with a mug of hot bortsch, the soup that had been their first course last night. The beetroot fumes were unbearable. Bent double, she just managed to reach the bathroom, where she was violently and disgustingly sick. She took a long time cleaning herself up, feeling shivery and wondering if she was going to be sick again. When she went back to bed, he had taken away the soup and left a plastic bowl.

'Can I get you anything?' he asked, his face drawn with concern.

'No, thank you. I'm sorry, I feel all churned up.'

'I'm the one who's sorry,' he said, sitting on the bed and holding her hand. 'Can't I do anything?'

'I think I'd better get some sleep,' she said.

The next day she was too weak to go to work. He rang Lindy for her. There was little else he could do except let her rest, but he cared for her with close attention. At about eleven in the morning the telephone went, and he, happening to be in her room, answered it by her bed rather than in the living-room.

'Hello?' he said. 'I'm afraid Belinda's not very well. She's

153

spending the day here in bed.' A pause. 'Well, thank you very much for inviting us but obviously we can't . . . I certainly will. Goodbye.'

'Who was that?' she asked.

'Ann-Louise. She was sorry to hear you're unwell and sends her best wishes. She wasn't sure where to find you during the day so she rang here.'

'What did she want?'

'She said someone at the office has given Hamish four tickets for tonight's performance at Covent Garden and they wondered whether we wanted to go.'

'That was nice,' she said. 'You could.'

'I've no desire to go to the opera.'

On the second day, a Saturday, she felt stronger and was able to spend most of the time in her dressing-gown. She found he had made an attempt to clean the kitchen. By his standards it was presentable.

'Thank you,' she said, feeling weepy. She thought that as far as the flat went, they had started down a slope at the bottom of which lay total squalor, but he had shown it was possible to scramble back towards decency. Maybe her illness had been a good thing, given him a jolt. There was nothing to be done about the cigarette burns on the sofa except invest in loose covers.

On Sunday, she was well enough to go out for a walk. It was a balmy spring day. 'Where would you like to go?' she asked him.

'Kensington Gardens. No, that would mean you had to drive.' His van needed a new clutch.

'I don't mind. It's been very boring for you, looking after me.'

They parked near Lancaster Gate and walked slowly, her arm in his, down the side of the water to Peter Pan.

'Symbol of eternal youth,' she smiled. 'When I was small and went to the pantomime, I couldn't understand why he was played by a girl.'

Tom frowned as if this still perplexed him. He could not

154

be sure what subjects might upset her. As his eyes wandered, he caught men staring at her and was reminded how ravishing she looked, and how envious he used to feel, when walking alone through a park, of a man with almost any girl. If he had seen Belinda, he would have watched her out of sight, and despaired of walking with a woman who came near her looks. Today she was wearing a shirt belonging to him, an ordinary thing transformed by her, and had tied her jersey round his neck.

'Shall we go and sit on a bench?' she asked, pulling him to turn up the grassy slope towards an equestrian statue.

'The sun's doing you good,' he said. She walked more vigorously, turned her face with eyes shut to its rays. Some of the trees were already breaking into leaf. They found a bench in the avenue to the left of the statue, sunny because the tree opposite it had been blown down.

'What was it you said about alteration?' she asked.

'I don't remember.'

'Yes you do. It was about love and alteration.'

'Oh that. I was forced to learn it as a punishment by a teacher called Chalky White. It put me off Shakespeare for years.'

'Can you still recite it?'

'I think so.' He knew so, having brushed it up for use on impressionable girls. He did not want to recite it now.

'Say it,' she said; shut her eyes again and waited.

'Let me not to the marriage of true minds
Admit impediments. Love is not love
Which alters when it alteration finds,
Or bends with the remover to remove:
O, no! it is an ever-fixed mark,
That looks on tempests and is never shaken;
It is the star to every wandering bark,
Whose worth's unknown, although his height be taken.
Love's not Time's fool, though rosy lips and cheeks
Within his bending sickle's compass come;

155

Love alters not with his brief hours and weeks,
But bears it out even to the edge of doom.
If this be error, and upon me prov'd,
I never writ, nor no man ever lov'd.'

She had slipped her hand into his. 'Thank you,' she said, and sat still. He would not disturb her by kissing her, though looking at her lips he wanted to. You are incorrigible, he told himself, not without satisfaction. She was relaxed. He felt restless, could not move the hand in which hers lay. Despite the expanse of ground before them, stretching to a hazy outline of Kensington Palace, there was something claustrophobic about being trapped on that bench.

He had once seen a couple copulating in broad daylight on a stretch of grass the other side of the trees from Park Lane. They were fairly discreet about it, you could only tell from their movements that they were doing more than kiss, while the spectators, scattered at various points of the compass, were positively surreptitious. One old man walked past the lovers twice, but each time as if by chance. The girl looked Persian, with long, black hair.

Today, most of the people walking in the park seemed foreign. It was, he supposed, a tourist attraction. Maybe the English went out of town at the weekend, if they wanted to walk. Yet the figure approaching them from the right looked English. A suspicion formed in Tom's mind. By the time he was sure, it was too late. He could no longer seize Belinda in his arms, as he would surely have been able to do in a movie, and by kissing her hide their faces. The movement would attract the walker, who strode forward rapidly but did not look as though he were noticing anyone. Tom shut his eyes and hoped the man would walk past.

Maybe Belinda felt herself being watched, or alarm was communicated via Tom's hand. She opened her eyes.

'David!' she said. He stopped in his tracks. In a few seconds, he would have been past them. He had only seen them a moment before and wanted to go. The sight was intolerable.

Tom made a show of waking up and saw the man standing a few yards away. He wore a check suit and striped tie, though not the bowler. He had been to lunch with his godmother, who had a house in Bayswater.

'Good afternoon,' David said to her. 'Are you all right?'

'Very well, thank you.'

'Good afternoon,' he said to Tom.

'Hi.'

Belinda loosed Tom's hand and put her arm round his shoulder.

'I'd like a word with you,' David said to Tom.

'No,' she said.

'I asked him.'

'Well,' Tom said, 'it seems Belinda would rather I stayed with her.'

'Are you treating her properly?'

'He's proposed to me,' Belinda said.

'You're not going to marry him!'

'I suppose she'll tell me when she's made up her mind,' Tom said.

'Yes, I will,' Belinda said. 'Isn't it the most heavenly day?'

'It won't last,' David asserted.

'Then we must enjoy it while we can,' she said.

'Goodbye,' he said to her. 'When you need me, you'll know where to find me.' He stumped off, unaware that he was marching back towards Bayswater. He was furious with himself for asking whether the pseudo-lodger and bogus table-lamp maker was treating her properly. A man like that was incapable of treating a woman properly. The question was what to do about it.

'Don't worry,' she said to Tom when he was gone. 'There's nothing he can do to come between us.'

Tom knew that on the contrary, David's intervention had driven them together. The antediluvian boor was imposing

157

his standards of conduct. Belinda had been a great help, mentioning the proposal.

In the following weeks he felt as though he were being taken over. She never nagged, her behaviour towards him was irreproachably sweet, but he found himself under pressure to make changes to his clothes, his hair, even the amount of wine he drank. Outwardly he was docile, because he could not be bothered to argue.

Belinda felt reassured by his willingness to oblige her. She knew he thought he drank just as much, but since they went to bed earlier, especially on the evenings she cooked, it must really be less. He tried to repay some of her kindnesses towards him, and whenever she asked him to recite the sonnet, he agreed.

Nineteen

The approach of the Chelsea Flower Show worried her.
Feeling remiss that she had stayed in London at Easter, she
went to Yorkshire for a weekend. She wanted to see her
father, who had been ill, and to find out whether her mother
was bound to visit London again so soon. The state of the
house emphasized the need for rigid economy.

'I thought I'd sell the books,' Mr Gould said to her when
they were sitting in his study after lunch. 'They got rather
damp last winter.'

'But you love your books.' Though he had talked for years
of selling them, chronic inertia, disguised as uncertainty
about how to get the best price, had prevented him.

'I barely look at them from one year to the next,' he said.

'You should find a house you can keep warm. For your
health, I mean.'

'Your mother says she'd rather not live in a rabbit hutch
and I'm inclined to agree with her. I don't think we'd get
much for this place.'

'It's a wonderful situation.'

'You've no idea how much a new roof costs now. I should
have spent the rest of my inheritance putting one on when
we arrived.'

'You didn't inherit much.'

'Virtually nothing. My father spent his money on my
mother's annuity and she died six months after him. Being

159

a twentieth-century bishop didn't pay, especially a twentieth-century colonial bishop. Which reminds me. Your mother greatly admired the wealth of your lodger's father. She went on about it for days.'

'You mean I should marry Tom?' she laughed, but really interested in the reply.

'How can I say? I haven't met him.'

'David dislikes him intensely.'

'That's a recommendation, though David would dislike any man closer to you than himself. I never said so at the time, but I didn't take to David.'

'I know you didn't, Daddy.'

'Do bring this lodger to stay. He couldn't be worse than David.'

'He's ten years younger than me.'

'You look quite young enough, I think.'

'And his father disapproves of him.'

'Good. We shall see more of you.'

'And he hasn't settled to a career.'

'I would advise you not to marry anyone excessively like me. For years I was going to give up the law, but I couldn't think what else to do.'

'I'm sure he'll succeed at something. It's just a question of what.'

Her mother entered with coffee. Belinda wondered how much more she might have said to her father. He had once remarked that he was keeping a certain picture to sell when he had to pay for her wedding. To get to their church you walked across a meadow. Ever since she could remember, she had imagined the procession across the meadow.

On Sunday night, in the train from Darlington to London, she realized she had been counting on her father, who had backed her refusal of David, to back her refusal of Tom. As for her mother, whose hostility she had at first taken for granted, Belinda could now see the explanation she would devise for the match: how Tom, whose father incidentally is a multimillionaire, came to lodge with her, and to everyone's surprise, including each other's, they just fell for each other, and he is a year or two younger, but what does it matter if you're in love?

Their life together had already become almost that of a married couple. He had quietened down. She knew he did all sorts of things to please her, while she was careful not to demand too much of him, and to see that he had nothing to complain of her as a woman. He was much more grown-up. To start with, he had felt so insecure that he was bound to be unreliable, but now that he knew she loved him, he could be himself. That was the wonderful thing about a loving relationship, the freedom it gave you to be yourself, without fear that your partner would find you inadequate or objectionable. You expressed your love by caring for each other, and she would crown her love for him by giving him a child. He was ready for fatherhood in a way which would have seemed impossible until these last weeks.

Being separated from him since Friday morning, when she left for work with her overnight bag, had helped clear her mind. It was in absence from the beloved, freed from the fever of desire, that you discovered your true feelings. All weekend she had wanted to telephone him, and hoped he might telephone her, but the tired fiction that she was the landlady, he the lodger, had restrained them. He would not have wanted to embarrass her in front of her parents.

Delight filled her when she had made up her mind. She ate some of her picnic. It was too big: her mother had pampered her. Belinda smiled. Tom still asked her to 'pamper' him when he wanted to make love, particularly when he wanted to lie back and enjoy her caresses. And he had pampered her, looking after her whenever she was tired, hungry or ill. Her illness had been the turning point. Since then, she had felt herself enclosed in a dream of content, not worrying about things but soothed by him, stimulated by him, amused by him. He had a good sense of humour. It made the perfect outlet for his unpredictability.

Her train hurtled south. She was approaching a state in which she believed all was for the best in the best of all possible worlds. How fortunate that her parents lived near to one of British Rail's fastest services, and that no engineering works, bane of Sunday travellers, were impeding her rush back to Tom. In a fortnight, her mother would travel up for the Flower Show. If he agreed, they could break the news then.

She was vexed that not everyone would see his good points, though nobody else, she admitted, had been given such close opportunities to observe them. If people criticized the engagement, they would in due course have to eat their words. Those stuffy types, most of them too unattractive to appeal to anyone, who thought sexual liberty was just a licence for men to take advantage of women, would be confounded.

At King's Cross, she caught a Piccadilly Line train. It was one of the better services on the Underground. She would be home sooner than if she had queued for a cab.

The flat was empty. He must have gone out before it got dark, as the living-room curtains were open. She switched on some lights before drawing them. In the kitchen, she noticed that the rack by the sink, which had been empty on Friday morning, contained a couple of plates. Having chosen a vase, she put the flowers she had brought from her parents' garden into water.

He had taken down his drawings of her. It made the room seem bare. She would ask him to put them up again.

In her bedroom, where she went to put her bag, there was an ash-tray next to the bed with several butts in it. That was a habit of which she had yet to cure him, leaving full ash-trays around the place. A stale smell was in the air. Here too he had tidied away his things.

The most likely explanation was that he had gone to see his mother at Canvey Island, the plan he had floated for Sunday, and had been persuaded to stay longer, or had trouble with the trains. She herself was remarkably punctual. It was only 10.30. She went back to the kitchen with a pot of homemade jam she had unpacked from her overnight bag, picked up the flowers and took them to the mantelpiece.

It was a stupid place to leave a note. She might not have found it for hours, lying there in front of some postcards and invitations. The one to Hamish and Ann-Louise's wedding, engraved on a stiff white card, stood just behind it.

She put down the vase and picked up the envelope. It bore her Christian name and the flourish with which he underlined things. He had written so little to her – a disadvantage of living together – that she would certainly keep this. Something fell to the bottom of the envelope. She opened it and shook. His set of keys slid out.

Curious, she unfolded the sheet of paper, one of the expensive ones he used for drawing, and read a letter so neat it must be a fair copy.

Dear Bel,

These are hard words to write and, I know, to get. I have been thinking over our future, and the more I think, the less I can see me making you happy. You have the wrong idea about me, as this behaviour of mine shows. You can't change me, and I can't change you (not that I would want to). It is less painful to make a clean break now, than for me to disappoint you later. I do believe this is in both our interests.

I have tried to say this to you a few times, but it was too difficult. I shall always look back on our time together as a taste of heaven on earth, but it could not last, as I think that deep down you knew too, when you did not reply to me.

With love and best wishes for the future,
Tom

PS I am sure you will soon find someone who deserves pampering more!

It was as if a boulder were falling from the sky, about to annihilate her. Quick as light she stepped aside. The letter was unbelievable. It could not be taken at face value. She was sad for Tom that he could have fallen so far beneath himself to write it. It was the most untruthful message she had ever had. The worst thing was that he left no telephone number, so she could not ring to correct him. She felt so angry that she found a pen and paper and started, as fast as her hand would move, to write a reply.

Dear Tom,

Since you didn't even have the decency to say in your note where you have gone, I am writing what I think of it in the hope that I can deliver this to you soon, in order to get my thoughts in order I am numbering them.

1. 'I have been thinking over our future'. Isn't that something we should do together?

2. How do you know I have the wrong idea about you? When we talk I think you will find I have a very good idea about you, probably better than you do yourself. Because of various factors you still don't understand.

3. Kindly don't lecture me on my 'interests' and I won't lecture you.

4. Since it was 'heaven on earth', don't you think it's worth trying to prolong? There's no point sacrificing the present to things which may happen in the future. I remember you even said that to me yourself once.

5. What do you mean, 'when I did not reply'? Are you trying to avoid saying that you proposed to me? I seem to remember that you said you were waiting for me to let you know. Well here's the answer. YES. I do want to marry you. I love you more than I've loved anyone ever before. I adore you, you're different to anyone else I've known and better. So stop confusing yourself about my 'not replying'. Here's my reply. I

*suppose we women, or this woman, is just a bit slower
than you are.*
  6. I will try to forget your PS. It is beneath contempt.
    With lots of love,
    Belinda XXX

She rocked back on her chair, reading the letter. She had
been sitting at the table to write it. It had relieved her
feelings slightly, but she still felt furious. She did not want
to look at his letter. It gave her a bad sensation.

The bell rang. She sat there. Waiting would teach him to
put his keys in the envelope. She was going to give him her
letter. It would clear the air. Like her illness, it would prove
a blessing in disguise. She could imagine how he would joke
about the rough phrases she had used.

The bell rang again. There was something desolate about
the prolonged sound. She folded her letter and went down
to the front door. Loosing the latch and looking triumphant
(there would be time later for forgiveness), she held out her
reply.

Hamish was taken aback, but not so much as she was.
He slowly raised his hand to take the paper, but she did not
let go of it.

'It's not for you,' she said.

'I'm sorry.'

'Whatever brings you here at this hour of the night?'

'Can I come up?'

'I suppose so.' It would be an awful nuisance if he were
there when Tom came back.

'You know what's happened?' he said when they were in
the living-room.

'Yes, I do. I'm treating it as a temporary aberration.'

'I'm afraid I don't think it's temporary. I think it's been
going on for some time.'

'I can't see what possible reason you could have for
thinking that. What do you know about me and him?'

'I found a note.'

165

'From Tom?'

'Yes.'

'Why was he writing to you?'

'It wasn't to me. I should like to add that I wasn't looking for it when I found it. It just fell out of a book Ann-Louise had been reading.'

'Show me.'

He passed it to her. It was the same sort of envelope as she had opened half an hour ago, taken from her own writing-case, and was underlined with the same flourish, but it bore the name 'Clarissa'. She turned it over in her hands.

'You'd better read it,' he said.

She took out a sheet of the drawing paper. His debased italic ran hurriedly down the page:

Darling Clarissa,

When am I going to see you again? I couldn't talk to you properly last night. I shall send this in another envelope via Ann-Louise at work, as she is the safest way I know of getting in touch with you. Don't you agree that she's extremely attractive? You and she might be identical twins.

If you are cross with me for writing, throw this letter away. If not, ring me during the day at the flat. We can't be boyfriend and girlfriend and not meet. It wouldn't be honest. So be a good girl and come and let me cook you lunch, if you have the time. You might bring your green skirt as it's given me the idea of a shade for my table-lamp. People have been a bit contemptuous about the lamp, but I assure you that a skilled user can expect satisfaction, especially after recent trials.

With all love from your boyfriend, waiting to be lit up by you.

T.

'I can't get this clear,' Belinda said, frightened at last.

'What it means is that under our very noses, at the party you gave when your mother was in London, your lodger took a shine to my fiancée.'

She considered his interpretation. 'You've got it the wrong way round,' she said. 'I had a long talk with Ann-Louise the weekend we stayed at your mother's house. She was after Tom then, even before he'd moved in here. She was utterly shameless. She wanted to swap him for you. The bitch just wanted to create the maximum possible havoc. She saw there was something between me and Tom at that dinner-party I gave, the night you told me she was thinking of becoming a Roman Catholic. Very funny. And there I was not liking her but thinking how brave she was not to mind looking how she does. It's because she's so skinny, she had to see if she could seduce Tom by wiggling her anorexic little bum at him.'

'Ann-Louise didn't write the letter.'

'But she did want to invite him for the weekend, didn't she! As my friend and supporter, of course, but so she could get her teeth into him. She's nothing but a common little tart. You're well rid of her.'

'She's not a tart and I love her.' He stopped the argument by starting to weep, a sight made more painful by his efforts to get a grip on himself.

'I should have a good cry,' Belinda advised, too shocked to cry herself. Like the return of a nightmare, she felt again the iron plate within her, its cord attaching her to Tom, wrenching at her heart. She would not be able to survive this. Already it was getting worse. Her whole body was starting to ache. The pain in her chest would become intolerable.

'Do you have anything to drink?' he asked.

'There's some Armagnac.' She had bought it as a present for Tom, who loved the stuff, but when she tilted the bottle over a glass a dribble came out. There had been plenty left on Thursday night.

The rubbish bin under the sink confirmed her suspicion. It contained the debris of a meal and an empty wine bottle. He had prepared food for her, they ate and on finishing the Armagnac they went away, kindly washing up their plates first. What a considerate touch. They only left a dozen other clues. If Ann-Louise had been there, Belinda would have thrown the bottle at her.

'I'm sorry, you'll have to have whisky instead,' she said, pouring one for herself too. She hurled the glass containing the thimbleful of Armagnac into the fireplace. It shattered with a satisfactory crash.

'Steady on,' Hamish said.

'How did you discover your little darling had got her claws into Tom?' she asked, sitting down.

'I went out this morning to do some research for the final interview, which is next weekend. She left me a note.'

'In which she said?'

'Words to the effect that we weren't suited and she'd decided to set up house with Tom Coleman. So sorry to have troubled me, at least we'd found out before we got married. What I can't get over is how long they'd been seeing each other. It makes everything she said to me seem meaningless.'

'They could have met here every day. She rang him once when I was ill. Tom concocted some story about opera tickets.'

'It's true we had the tickets, but we'd agreed not to invite you. She said you couldn't be asked without Tom, I said I really didn't want to see him.'

'He was so naïve.'

'Naïve! I'd like to wring his neck. If it wasn't for him I'd still have Ann-Louise. I've never seen a more blatant sponger. How much rent did he pay you? How much? Not a penny, I bet. It suited him to live in your nice, comfy flat for a while, add you to his little list of conquests and move on before the whole thing got serious. You're the lucky one.'

'He wanted to marry me.'

'Really.'

'Nobody will believe me when I tell them.'

'The thing is, you hadn't sent out the invitations.'

'Go to hell, Hamish.'

'At least you haven't got to ring up your mother and say you're awfully sorry, the whole thing's off.'

'At least you're not late with your period.'

'You haven't?'

'Let him get me pregnant? I don't know. I've been a bit careless, that's all. Time to go to the chemist and buy one of those kits.'

'Oh my God.'

'It's probably a false alarm.'

'To think I was worrying about my political future.'

'From that point of view, I'd have thought it was a great help to have got rid of Ann-Louise.'

'It only means I've got to find another fiancée by Saturday, for the final interview.'

'I'll impersonate her. I don't see why the bitch should ruin your political future.'

'I couldn't possibly trouble you.'

'It doesn't show yet I'm an unmarried mother, does it?'

'No.'

'But you think that in the party of family values, it would be a bit much to pass me off as your future wife.'

'Victor would know you weren't.'

'I thought you were his candidate.'

'He has promised me his support.'

'Then he won't expose you. Added to which, I doubt whether a broken engagement worries him.'

'Maybe not. To tell the truth, I couldn't care less about him. It's Central Office who won't forgive me if I back out now. I'm their man to beat the racist. But even that doesn't worry me as much as the falseness between you and me.'

'In politics, I'm told, one has to endure a bit of falseness.'

'I've always admired you.'

'I can't think why, I'm going from bad to worse. Do you

know the proverb about me? My father's mother was very beautiful and terrifyingly devout. I'm supposed to take after her, though devout isn't quite the word and I'm sure she was better looking. When any man but her husband praised her looks, she replied: "As a jewel of gold in a swine's snout, so is a fair woman which is without discretion." My father said it was awful. She thought she was being modest, but she made it sound as if a swine had propositioned her.'

'Oh dear.'

'Not that I think you're a swine.'

'Thanks.'

'Hamish, may I ask you something, as an old friend?'

'Of course.'

'Will you hold me?'

As soon as he sat down beside her on the sofa and placed an arm round her, she collapsed in a fit of weeping. Nobody could replace Tom, yet such an intense loneliness was left that she would rather anyone was there.

In a few minutes she found herself feeling the opposite. It was no good. Hamish could do nothing for her. She wished herself dead. She had brought this last humiliation on herself and would rather not burden her friends.

Hamish was troubled by stirrings of desire which distracted him from his own sorrow, and from sympathy with Belinda.

The doorbell rang.

Twenty

Hamish made as if to answer it, but she restrained him. She could not stop herself hoping. Half the adaptability on which the human race prides itself is the refusal to admit things have changed. We cannot believe that the person we love will never again walk into the room, or telephone, or write. Grief is at first survived because we have not adapted.

'Go away,' she said, unutterably tired, when she saw David on the doorstep.

'I came to see if I could help.'

'It's too late.'

'Can't I come in for a moment? I presume Hamish is here.'

'He'll be going soon.'

'Please let me in. I need to talk to him.'

'I haven't the energy to argue,' she said, and shut the door in his face.

'Who was it?' Hamish asked.

'David. So thoughtful of you to ask him.'

'I didn't. He rang me this evening and I told him what had happened. Not that I wanted to.'

'You might have guessed he'd take the slightest excuse to run round here. Anyhow, he wants one of his famous words with you. If you hurry, you'll catch him.'

'Isn't there anything I can do for you?'

'Nothing.'

He was hurt by her loss of interest in him.

'Well, goodbye,' he said. 'We'll keep in touch.'

By waiting, he prompted her to give him a perfunctory kiss on the cheek. She saw him to the door of the flat and he went downstairs. David was striding up and down the pavement.

'Come and sit in my car,' he said. Hamish unwillingly acquiesced. 'Now brief me. Does she know where they've gone?'

'She didn't even know who he'd gone with.'

'That doesn't surprise me. Where do you think they are?'

'Most likely they've gone back to the place Ann-Louise was living before.'

'Where was that?'

'She shared a flat with someone called Helen Gordon.'

'Where?'

'Something like 7 Pullinger Street. But so what? I can't stop her if she wants to run off with a bastard.'

'I don't see why he should be allowed to get away with it.'

'As I said to Belinda, I'd happily wring Coleman's neck. But one can't condone neck-wringing.'

'You may take that attitude. As a friend of Belinda, I don't.'

'Perhaps you want to force Coleman to keep his word to her?'

'I want him to suffer for breaking it.'

'The best thing you could do is forget about them both. I don't wish to be tactless, but the last time you intervened on her behalf you nearly ended up in court. Revenge isn't just illegal. Belinda wouldn't want you to do anything to Tom on her behalf.'

'Have you asked her?'

'No, but she thinks Ann-Louise was more to blame than he was.'

'Exactly. She doesn't know the first thing about it. The pair of you are both at liberty to act in a totally supine way, but I shall do as I please. What right has she to order me about when she won't even talk to me?'

'She was exhausted. Don't you understand, David, that you're putting yourself on the level of a football hooligan?'

'They're the last of us with any vigour. You want a deodorized country where we go shopping in bland new stores with canned music or, in one per cent of cases, stay at home listening to string quartets, and either way never care enough about anything to raise our voices. Young men need to fight. We don't do any fighting so what do we do? We get obsessed by sex but reduce it to triviality. The Greeks spent ten years besieging Troy after Paris carried off Helen.'

'Wasn't she someone else's wife?'

'You wouldn't have lifted a finger if Ann-Louise had been yours.'

'Nowadays we don't take so dim a view of divorce. Nor do we think we have to behave like primitive Greek tribesmen, showing our heroism by going off and getting killed. Maybe we should, but an individual can't start living by a code which is at odds with everyone else's. Not if it involves killing.'

'You've the soul of a chartered accountant.'

'Just what Burke said. Every age takes too low a view of itself, though every age is in danger of going back, as they say of land which falls out of cultivation. We could go back to narrow-minded nationalism. Parts of the Islamic world have gone back to religious bigotry. You, if I may say so, seem to be going back to the jungle.'

'You're also rather like a civil servant, aren't you? Always thinking up bloodless reasons why things can't be done.'

'Will you promise me one thing?'

'That I won't interfere?'

'Yes.'

'No.'

'I'm going home. If it relieves your feelings to rant against life, by all means rant.'

'Stop being so wet, Hamish.'

'It's not wet to believe in gradual change. Your fantasies are the real wetness. You can't accept the world as it is so you pretend that if only men were more violent things would change for the better. They wouldn't.'

'That's a travesty.'

'I hope so. Good night.'

David was left sitting in his car. He saw Hamish drive away from a space fifty yards down the street. It shook him to think that such a spineless character might become an MP. The fellow was amiable enough, but symbolized the degeneracy of Britain. Under gross provocation, he had decided to take no action whatever; to hide his cowardice by claiming it was uncivilized to hit someone. This was what put civilization in danger, the gutless refusal to teach barbarians like Tom Coleman a lesson.

The road was deserted. David looked up Pullinger Street in his A-Z map of London, could not find it. That was the limit. His friend had given him a non-existent address. He had come all the way to Hammersmith to offer help to a girl who refused to let him in, and a man who lied to him. Helen Gordon might, however, be in the phone book.

By taking Coleman into her bed Belinda had shown herself unworthy. He almost hated her for consuming so much of his time; was filled with boundless exasperation with her, and with himself for letting her dominate his life. His previous delusions, that she would be grateful if he beat up her seducer, and that gratitude would make her fall in love, were overlaid by a new and worse madness, that her opinion did not matter. She had the brain of a pea. It was as if he had fallen in love with a shop girl, a sweet creature but infinitely dim. If she wanted him to leave Coleman alone, she was wrong. She knew nothing. He alone knew the horror of the world and the necessity of fighting it.

Hamish drank another glass of whisky when he got home, managed to go to sleep, but woke two hours later. He knew as he regained consciousness that something terrible had happened. She could not have done this if she had realized how he would feel it. She must have closed her eyes to that. From early on, her toughness had alarmed him. Things did not touch her, or if they did, she would not show it. He thought a miracle had occurred when she accepted him.

When Belinda awoke, she was perturbed to find how long she had slept. It did not seem right. She could, however, reassure herself that she felt in despair. Everything was for the worst. She would sink deeper into depression, become less and less capable of taking good decisions, or any decisions at all, lose her flat and her friends, as she had already lost her love. That was what happened when you got old. You became, at most, an adventure for a younger man, who afterwards ran off with a younger woman. Two of the butts in the ash-tray by her bed were marked with the younger woman's lipstick. Ann-Louise must have enjoyed leaving that evidence of her triumph. If she'd had more time, she would have carved her initials on the bedside table.

Belinda telephoned the people for whom she was supposed to be working that morning. They were annoyed to hear she was staying at home. When she rang the agency there was an edge of vexation in Lindy's voice. Some of the firm's best clients had complained and it might not be possible to get another placing until next week. Belinda did not feel up to explaining what had gone wrong. She remembered the excuses she heard when she was working with Lindy. Whether a girl said she was ill, or going through a crisis with her boyfriend, the advice one usually wanted to give was: 'Pull yourself together. You're not really ill/he isn't really worth it. You'll feel worse if you hang around at home.'

The kit showed she was pregnant. She believed this

already: it was silly to think she needed science to tell her. She felt unable to have one constructive thought, wished she had gone to work. All she could do was extrapolate from present trends and foresee disaster for herself. She was sick of London. She wanted to go and hide herself in a cottage in the country with her child and a couple of Labradors; wondered how much the cheapest part of this arrangement, the puppies, would cost.

Life would be easier to bear if Tom were dead. Then it would be natural for him to be inaccessible. Knowing he was alive, yet as separate from her as if he had been buried, made the pain indescribable. Time was supposed to heal, but she would have their baby to remind her of him.

That was another difficulty she had courted like a giggling teenager who knew no better. Perhaps she hadn't giggled enough when she was a teenager, so her eventual loss of control was more complete. The risk of conceiving the baby had increased her need to trust him. Her love had grown so strong that it seemed impossible he should fail to return it.

On Tuesday morning, with an excitement she knew to be unfounded, she went downstairs to see if there were any letters. These unbidden hopes would last for years. She was too early. The post had not yet come. Later she found letters from her bank and David.

There are few things more horrible than a polite letter from a bank. This one said the bank thought she would like to know she had exceeded her credit limit. Would she please remit funds immediately, or get in touch to discuss the situation. A chart was enclosed to help her work out her average monthly expenditure by adding up what she spent on housing, transport, food, etc. Tom must come under entertainment. She could not face talking over her affair, or affairs, with someone else. They would make it sound so easy to have insisted on his paying rent and a share of the bills.

When she had drunk several cups of tea and given up

trying to eat some cereal, she supposed she might look at David's letter.

Dear Belinda,

Thank you for shutting the door in my face last night. I know this may seem a strange thing to write, but it made me realize how little my help means to you. If I am drawing the wrong conclusion, please let me know. I would always want to be of help to you, but if I hear nothing, I shall assume you have no guidance to offer me, and shall feel free to act on my own initiative.

I do hope everything works out as you hope. It may interest you to know that I shall not be getting the regiment. I am taking this opportunity to leave the army and travel.

Please get in touch with me if you want me to help.
With love,
David

Another hand-washing exercise, she thought. Nothing would induce her to ask David for help. Her wounds were too raw, her stupidity too conspicuous, for her to ask anyone for help, but she could see a day when she would regret that David had forgotten her. There was only one thing worse than being troubled by men.

She was almost pleased, on Wednesday morning, to be asked by Hamish to have dinner with him that evening.

177

Twenty-One

Hamish insisted on picking her up from her flat. He said that otherwise he would have nobody to drink with, as she would bring her car and refuse alcohol.

'You've brought yours,' she said.

'I'm not so law-abiding.'

'But you should be if you intend to make the laws.'

'The police have got this drink-driving thing out of proportion. It's counter-productive. Even if they stamp out drunken driving, they will lose a disproportionate amount of goodwill, quite apart from the time they waste when they ought to be catching criminals.'

'That's a saloon bar attitude.'

'Do-gooders spend too little time in bars.'

'How fierce you are tonight, Hamish.'

'Events have taught me to be radically normal. I'm daring to be more and more conventional. I do not offer the Tories of the Thames estuary a *bien-pensant* programme. Victory in life comes from exaggerating your strength, by concentrating your forces. What have I to exaggerate? My normality.'

'It isn't normal to be all that normal.'

'For the purposes of talking to you, I must be understood to be sending myself up.'

His mood was bizarre. Obviously he did not want to talk about anything painful until they reached the restaurant.

He had chosen an Italian place. The proprietor showed them to their table, asked what they would have to drink. Belinda ordered a kir, Hamish a large whisky. He broke open the packet of bread sticks on the table and offered her one.

'What did your test say?' he asked.

'It was positive.'

'How do you feel about that?'

'Pleased.' She was more and more pleased. Something good had come out of the débâcle.

'An abortion is, I hope, out of the question?'

'I couldn't.'

'Splendid.'

'I didn't know you felt strongly about it. I thought the inconvenience of having a baby would strike you. When you're an MP, you must speak up for unmarried mothers.'

'No cause will be nearer my heart. They have a terrible time. In all but a minority of cases, the unmarried mother is placed in a dilemma. Either she stays at home to look after her child, but is condemned to poverty and, quite likely, isolation, or she looks for a job. But if she finds one, apart from the fact that it is likely, assuming she has no professional qualifications, to be badly paid, she has to make arrangements for her child, including the child when sick, or after school, or during the holidays. These commitments further limit the range of jobs she can apply for. She may have to spend large sums on child-minders, and know that for all the expense, the arrangements are second best. Her own mother may be able to help, but if so, apart from the risk of friction between mother and daughter, this arrangement limits where the daughter can live. She may, moreover, worry as her child grows up that the absence of a father is detrimental. She also has the strain of taking major decisions about the child's future on her own. Just after the birth, she has no partner to help her through the post-natal depression she may feel.'

'No need to rub it in.'

'Shall we order?' They studied their menus and told a waiter what they would like. Hamish also asked for wine and mineral water.

'So what's your solution to the problem of unmarried motherhood?' she asked.

'Marriage.'

'Very practical.'

'It's better than giving unmarried mothers more money. That would increase the supply of them, but their incomes would still be too low.'

'I'm sure eligible bachelors, undeterred by our shop-soiled condition, are queuing up to marry us. They don't mind being fathers to other men's children. I think if I had a proposal like that I'd suspect the man's motives. I'd be back to my old condition of not wanting any man who wanted me. You don't realize how ghastly most men are. Baby and I would rather stay huddled over the gas ring in our bed and breakfast room. That reminds me, where are they living?'

'With her friend Helen. Am I ghastly?'

'Not especially. If you could give me the address and telephone number.'

He let her have the correct information. 'David was in such a bloodthirsty mood I made up a false address.'

'He sent me a letter offering to help.'

'You could ask him to marry you. I'm sure he would.'

'I'm not that desperate.'

'He may be.'

'He said in his letter he would feel free to act on his own initiative if he didn't hear from me.'

'Leave him to it. I now wish to outline the reasons why I want to marry you.'

'Are you proposing?'

'Yes.'

'You can't do it like that.'

'I know it's not romantic, but I failed at romance. Even

if I'd proposed to Ann-Louise in a hot-air balloon, I don't think she would have stayed with me.'

'There are forms of words.'

'Which you wouldn't believe, if I used them three days after my last fiancée ran off.'

'Exactly. It's much too soon.'

'You look adorable when you're running away. I want to pursue you through the spring woods and when, your eyes shining, your bosom panting, your golden locks disordered, you turn at bay against the young leaves, looking unutterably beautiful, I want to take your hand and on bended knee swear undying love.'

'That's better. Why didn't you tell me this before?'

'Because everyone else was telling you and I thought I was too dull to stand a chance.'

'So now I'm down on my luck the bores will start to prey on me.'

'Some of them always have, but this bore had the tact to keep his mouth shut.'

'What reasons were you going to offer for opening it?'

'I had them neatly set out, but you tainted my logic with love.'

'Decontaminate yourself.'

'I remember. I was going to declare my interests. First there's the motive which vulgar and unromantic people use the word "rebound" to describe, as in "He married her on the rebound." I can't stand being by myself again. Next, acceptance by you would mitigate the extreme embarrassment of losing Ann-Louise. Third, I need a fiancée by Saturday, and know you'd make a good impression on the selection committee. Last, although you couldn't be as conventional as I am, you want a husband, and at least you know me, and might judge me a better bet than some; and I know you and think the same.'

'There must be more to it than that.'

'You're also incredibly sexy.'

'I'm a mother.'

'A young mother, full of vitality and love. Just right for a jaded politician.'

'But my child!'

'I would regard the child as mine, as if you and I had been having a pre-marital affair. Virtually nobody knows how close you and Tom were and the child won't be born until after we're married, which must improve the chances of me and baby getting on. What pudding would you like?'

A trolley had been wheeled up.

'I'm rather full,' she said.

'You must eat properly. How about some figs?'

'All right.'

'Profiteroles for me.'

'If you call this normal behaviour, I don't know what you'd mean by abnormal.'

'It's normal enough to marry, or avoid marrying, for practical reasons. The only unconventional thing I've done is give them out loud. I admit I've been a little dishonest, by making too little of the fact that I'm in love with you. But so what if I love you? You inspire that emotion in plenty of men. My advantage isn't that I love you more, though I think I do. It's that I know you're in difficulties, and can claim to be in a better position to help.'

'If you saw an attractive girl drowning in a river, would you make her promise you a good screw before you pulled her out?'

'Certainly not.'

'That's your attitude to me. I'm in trouble so you think you can get a replacement fiancée at a bargain-basement price. You assumed I was beyond your means so fixed yourself up with an emaciated chick instead, but when, to your surprise, she said you couldn't have her, you suddenly heard I'd become vulnerable. Off you rushed to promise me twenty years of free child care if only I'd marry you.'

'Actually I rang you up to ask you out to dinner.'

'You're cautious. To maximize your chances, you gave me a few drinks before submitting your bid. You also reminded me what bliss it is being an unmarried mother, as if I hadn't thought of that. Go on. I can see you think I need another reminder. "Think of your child," you want to say, just like they say "Think of your shareholders" in the City. What a coup. Instead of spending months wooing me, only to see me go off on someone else's arm, you can nip in smartly and secure me in the course of an evening. How your mother would approve, not that you mentioned her in your little list of motives. Belinda is such a nice girl, Mummy will think, she is one of us, a more than fit replacement for sour little Ann-Louise, unlike her she doesn't have a career, looks better at child-bearing too, a Sloane Ranger with just enough wit to see which side her bread is buttered. It will be a pleasure to patronize her, because, though we never mention it, her parents are poorer than us and Hamish got her out of a scrape.'

He was so stolid he waited before saying: 'It isn't like the attractive girl in the water. Screwing her wouldn't help, whereas I thought marrying you would. But I don't want to argue. I'm sure I've behaved atrociously.'

There was a long silence while they sipped their coffee.

'I expect I have too,' she said. 'I'm sorry, I feel so overwrought I wouldn't know a happy ending if I saw one. I think I'll go.'

'Let me run you home.'

'No, thanks.'

'In that case we'll get the restaurant to ring for a cab. You might walk for miles.'

She got up. 'Thanks for dinner,' she said. 'Let me know what time you want to leave for the interview on Saturday.'

He considered going after her, but the whole restaurant would stare at them and he hadn't paid the bill. Instead he tried to look as though he expected her to leave. Was that a last jibe about the interview, or the honouring of her original offer – or a sign of regret at being so outspoken? Hamish thought the fundamentals of the deal were so strong he had no cause for despair.

Twenty-Two

The street where Tom had gone to live was not in Islington but a nondescript region on the further side, Stoke Newington perhaps. It was loud with traffic. Belinda arrived at noon the next day and left her car in a side street. She found the door to the flat beside a fish and chip shop and pressed a grimy bell; could not hear above the noise of the lorries whether it rang. Her assumption was that Ann-Louise and Helen would both have gone to work. Perhaps he had gone out too, for nobody came.

'Hi!' She spun round and saw him holding a carrier bag. He looked well. 'Come on up,' he said, unlocking the door.

The main room of the flat seemed almost as noisy as the street. It shook when a heavy vehicle passed. The furniture was decrepit.

'Coffee?' he asked her. 'I've just been to get some milk.'

'Thanks.' His bag looked as though it also contained whatever he was going to cook for Ann-Louise tonight.

'If I'd known you were coming I'd have asked you to bring one or two things I forgot,' he shouted from a sort of cupboard, which served as kitchen.

'I did bring something of yours,' she said, when he came back in and sprawled on a beanbag. 'Ours, I mean.'

'What's that?'

'I'm pregnant.'

'Yours.'

Looking back on the conversation, she would have liked to leave then, if only she had been stronger, or her love weaker. Maybe it was right to give him the chance to act differently. She could at least use that reason for her journey, though she knew him too well to hold out any sincere hope the pregnancy would change his mind. But once he reacted with his usual selfishness, dispute was useless. Arguing is a less abject form of protest than begging, but it may indicate the same reluctance to accept the truth.

'Undoubtedly ours,' she replied.

'Look. I didn't ask you to get pregnant. You chose to.'

'I was just a bit forgetful, that's all.'

'Never mind. You can get rid of it.'

'I don't want to get rid of him or her.'

'All right, but don't try to bother me with it. You just do whatever you want.'

'You mean you won't even want access to the baby?'

'Jesus, no. My old man got married when he put a bun in my mother's oven. What a blunder.'

'If your mother had aborted you, you wouldn't exist.'

'Who'd be around to mind?' he laughed.

'She would.'

'Her life was messed up by having me.'

'How can you say that? You're not wicked but you deliberately harden your heart. You don't want to hear what's right because you're afraid it might be inconvenient. You must be the weakest person I've ever known.'

'Whereas it's the height of altruism to get yourself pregnant and then expect someone to marry you.'

She sat with her head in her hands. It was so odd to be in the same room as him without any physical contact. They might be addressing each other from opposite sides of a ravine.

'You've got a terrible outlook,' she said. 'You just don't realize.'

'Thanks for coming to tell me that interesting fact. I thought I might see the Galloping Major but I didn't expect to see you. I don't deserve a visit from the wronged woman.'

'David will certainly try to get you,' she said.

'I always thought he should be locked up.'

'Goodbye,' she said, rising to her feet. 'I never imagined you could fall so low. Still, you've found a lovely spot to live.'

He wondered whether to mention that he had left behind his slippers, the embroidered ones Corinna Eliot gave him. They must still be under the bed. He feared he must give up all hope of seeing them again, but at the last moment he rushed across the room and stood between her and the door.

'We oughtn't to part as enemies,' he said. The vainglory of his new scheme made it hard to think. Just imagining it made him feel bloated with pride.

'Don't demean yourself any more,' she warned, guessing his intention.

'There's nobody here,' he said. 'You look marvellous today.'

She forced aside the atrocious idea of paying back Ann-Louise.

'For old times' sake,' he said.

'You know who you remind me of?'

'Who?' he asked, approaching her.

'Conrad.'

He stopped.

'Except that Conrad admitted there was something wrong with himself whereas you don't even realize.'

He turned away, imagining the terms in which he would describe this encounter to Ann-Louise. 'Belinda came and tried to drag me onto a higher moral plane,' he would say.

When she got home, she wept, marvelling that she had not done so earlier; then attempted, far sooner than was practicable, to feel pleased. He had made everything so clear. If he had given any sign that the baby would bring him back, she could not have accepted Hamish. Now, however, there was no excuse for being uncertain herself.

She telephoned his office. 'I'm sorry, he's in a meeting,' a secretary said. 'Can I take a message?'

'Please could you say the bid he made on Wednesday has been accepted.'

'What was that for?'

'Gould. You can add that he's made a superb acquisition and all of us at Gould and Company will be doing our best to ensure he never regrets it. This is a former market leader who embarked on an unwise programme of diversification and is therefore showing – not to say feeling – her age. Analysts believe, however, that new management should be able to return the business to long-term profitability.'

'Could you say that a bit more slowly?'

'Just tell him Belinda says yes.'

Twenty-Three

They allowed ample time on Saturday morning to get to
the selection meeting. She drove while Hamish ran over his
speech. A few miles before their destination, they stopped
in a lay-by, on a short stretch of road between two suburbs.

He went into a field and relieved himself. She slid over
into the passenger seat.

'I think we ought to wait here a few minutes,' he said,
getting back in. 'Otherwise we'll be early.' The proceedings
would unfold at one of the constituency's Conservative
Clubs; started with a buffet lunch at which the four candidates and their partners, if any, were to mingle with members of the special executive committee. This body included,
in addition to the original selection committee, three rep-
resentatives from each of the eleven wards. Its task was to
choose the winner from a short list of four.

'Is there anything else I need to remember?' she asked.
She felt less worried than he did because to her the occasion
was unimportant. She did not want to let him down, but
she couldn't care which way the verdict went.

'Is the ring still hurting?' he asked.

'Don't worry.' To confirm her status she wore a diamond
engagement ring, painfully tight on her finger. It was a
Stuart heirloom which Ann-Louise had spurned in favour
of one bought specially.

'You look perfect,' he said. There had been no danger

that his new fiancée would spring a fluorescent green skirt on the selectors. Her blue, two-piece outfit reminded him of one he had seen the Prime Minister wearing. Belinda was beautiful – that was unavoidable – but not ostentatious. The women on the committee would have no cause to feel that the girl from the metropolis had tried to outshine them. They should be flattered by the imitation, while the men would be captivated.

'I've never seen that tie,' she said.

'Cedric insisted on polyester. One thing is not to look too confident. There ought to be a respectful nervousness about us. This is a day when the rank and file are entitled to feel significant, but it won't do any harm if we suggest that as far as we're concerned, they will always come first. Not that we must be too obvious.'

'Right.'

'Remember if anyone asks we're getting married on the twenty-fourth of July.'

'I've got that.' She had also been taught the value of phrases such as 'I think we all worry sometimes that we may be swamped.'

'Let's go,' he said, as though they were parachuting into enemy territory.

The club's main room was entered straight from the pavement, through a wooden porch attached to the inside of the front door. A large bar jutted from the wall opposite. To the left stood a pool table, to the right a dartboard. Neither was in use, but a man in a threadbare blazer, regimental badge on the breast pocket, was trying his luck on a fruit machine. The low ceiling and shortage of natural light made the place seem smaller than it was. There were already about forty people, slightly more men than women, most with glasses in their hands.

The constituency chairman greeted Hamish and Belinda. He was a bald, gloomy fellow who had retired some years ago from the police force. Hamish had met him before, and most of the paunchy circle of men talking to him, but Belinda was glad to spy Victor Coleman breezing towards her. Though dressed like a spiv, he had a strong look of his son. She moved over to meet him. All links with Tom were valuable.

'So, we can put you on our leaflets after all,' he said. He had been warned by Hamish that Belinda had replaced Ann-Louise. 'That should help. Come over here and we'll get you a drink. What will it be? Don't say mineral water.'

'You're as bad as Hamish. One of us will have to drive home, you know.'

'We'll make sure you're in no state to do that. Let's call it gin and tonic. Then I'll introduce you to a few of our people. You'll find out what the animals at the zoo have to put up with.'

Men and women came to peer at her. Conversation could be a little forced. Praise for the sandwiches, sausage rolls and cakes, which various of the ladies had made, was a reliable topic.

'How does our organization compare to yours?' a woman asked her.

'I'm very impressed, though of course I haven't got a great deal to compare it with yet,' Belinda said, fearing questions about her local constituency association. She had forgotten the name of her MP.

'Do you go out to work, then?'

'I had a job, but once we're married, we're very much hoping to start a family, and I think my main role will be to look after the children and give Hamish the back-up he needs.'

'What do you think about coming to live in the sticks, then?'

'I certainly wouldn't call this the sticks. I think what makes any place is its people, so it would really be very easy to settle in here.' Did that sound presumptuous? 'Frankly it would be rather a relief to get out of London.'

'That's what we found. You'd hardly recognize the place, not since the war. Might as well be in Calcutta.'

'The pace of change is rather frightening,' she said. 'I wish things hadn't happened so fast.'

'Who asked us whether we wanted all those people? Enoch said what was happening, but who listened to Enoch? Ted tried to gag Enoch. What sticks in my craw is the press won't even report what we think.'

Belinda found she need say nothing. She stood with a concerned expression on her face while a group of them explained their anxieties. They seemed to regard her as an emissary from official Britain who could take their story back and spread it. The speakers reassured each other that their views were acceptable, and that they knew what roles Enoch, Ted and Maggie had played.

'Know Eric Wright, do you?' one of them asked.

'I don't think I do.'

'Came down here and gave a super little talk on racial differentiation. Not everyone wanted to invite him, but if it's a private club we can invite who we like, can't we?'

'It's a free country,' she said.

At last lunch ended and the candidates were asked to withdraw. They were taken upstairs by a party member who had volunteered to look after them, but grumbled that he was missing the fun. Although Belinda had glimpsed Hamish's rivals, she had not spoken to any of them yet. In the little room where they waited, sitting among piles of stickers saying 'Vote Williams' and beneath framed photographs of Winston Churchill and Margaret Thatcher, she was able to study them. They could even hold a stilted conversation.

Victor had said two candidates were there just to make up the numbers. One of these had been member for a Welsh seat, and a junior minister in the Welsh Office, before losing to Labour. His wife was friendly. She and Belinda knew some of the same people. The other was a smooth young man who had been President of the Oxford Union and said he was amazed to have got this far, though he had fought a seat last time. He was alone.

The dangerous character was also young. Kevin Bandall looked as if he had never been out of doors, but sat all his life in sunless rooms hatching plots. His views on immigration were known to be virulent. At the last election he had fought a seat near to Hamish's in Lancashire, but he had the immense advantage of being born and brought up in the constituency they were now contesting, where it was said he had falsified his date of birth in order to become an under-age member of the Young Conservatives. His girlfriend shared his paleness. She looked like a disenchanted lavatory cleaner. This was clearly the most important day of her life. Belinda remembered seeing a contingent of young members keeping themselves to themselves. They must be Kevin's claque.

Each candidate had to go downstairs, deliver a ten-minute speech and answer questions. The order was alphabetical, which meant that Hamish was last. Kevin and his companion went first. At one point a distant cheer could be heard. Talk flagged. The waiting-room was hot. They came back, the girl looking pleased.

Neither of the others received applause which was audible upstairs. Belinda had already started to think more highly of her fiancé. With the possible exception of the ex-junior minister, he was clearly the best of the bunch.

She and Hamish were put with the chairman at a trestle table placed at one end of the room, facing the members of the special executive committee on chairs arranged in rows. The bar was still open. Victor was standing at the back in one corner, watching. The chairman told Hamish he was to speak for ten minutes on how he would represent the constituency in Parliament.

Belinda was astonished how good he was. He had no notes. He sounded sincere, forceful, unpatronizing. His view on the death penalty – 'We have got to have it back [applause] in the first instance for terrorists and for those who murder policemen' [further applause, in which the chairman joined] – went down extremely well. So did his remarks about 'England for the English'.

'But I will be honest with you,' he concluded. 'If you do

me the honour, and it is a very great honour, of sending me as your representative to Westminster, I cannot promise you that the world will be changed overnight. I cannot promise you that all the things we would like to see done will be done tomorrow. But I can promise you that the voice of this constituency will be heard loudly and clearly where it matters most. I am reminded of that line from G. K. Chesterton which goes, "For we are the people of England, that never have spoken yet." We are indeed the people of England. We have defended this country through two world wars, and through countless tribulations since. Let the people of England now speak, and let us see that we prevail.'

She could not make a direct comparison between the applause Hamish received and that gained by Kevin, but she was sure her man had won. He contrived to look natural as their representative, the man who not only knew how they felt but would make their feelings intelligible to Parliament. She thought she had been unfair to politicians as a class. It was an art, to discover what the people think and put it better than they can themselves, guiding their impulses into good channels and filtering out such poisons as racial prejudice.

Hamish was asked some questions, which he handled perfectly.

'Will you and your wife be living here?' was the last.

'Belinda and I' – he smiled down at her, she back at him – 'would without doubt make our home here if you were to choose me to be your MP. I ought really to say if you were to choose us, for she is as much involved in this as I am' – another fond smile – 'and I know there is nowhere she would rather bring up children than in this thriving English community.' Don't overdo it, she thought, but he had them eating out of his hand. They did not think to ask at what age he intended to remove his children from their thriving English community in order to send them to schools in parts of the country, and in company, which he found even more agreeable.

As the applause died down, a buzzing was heard. Victor, who had been clapping as loudly as anyone, took a portable telephone out of his pocket and retired from the room. The chairman thanked Hamish and Belinda, asking them to go back upstairs while the ballot was held. At the bottom of the stairs, next to a pile of beer crates, Victor was conducting his conversation. He motioned to them to wait.

'I'll be there as soon as I can,' he said. 'I'm leaving now.'

'What's happened?' she asked in alarm.

'Tom's had an accident. He may be dying. I've got to go.'

'I'm coming too,' she said.

'You can't!' Hamish protested. 'What will I tell them in there?'

'That I've been taken ill.'

'We'll go out the back,' Victor said, leading the way.

She did not look round. Hamish slowly climbed the stairs to rejoin the others. 'Belinda's not very well,' he said, and sat down. The wife of the ex-junior-minister, who neither expected nor wanted her husband to win the nomination, asked if she could help.

'No, thank you. Someone's looking after her.'

Kevin's girlfriend, who had thought from the first that the blonde bombshell was devoid of political commitment, felt sure Hamish was lying.

'Who's looking after her?' she demanded.

'A kind member of the association,' Hamish said mildly.

'Victor Coleman, I bet. You and she are in his pocket.'

The man looking after them was unequal to this disruption, so the ex-junior-minister intervened. 'I say, we can't start arguing among ourselves. We've got to wait for the result.'

'If he wins it's been rigged,' she said. 'Kevin had all the votes he needed until Coleman started canvassing for Stuart. At least three members of the committee do business with Coleman.'

'Don't be so ridiculous,' Hamish said.

'Hark at the public schoolboy,' she cried. 'Let's keep it

all in the club, he says. If you think I'm going to let some rich carpetbagger do Kevin out of a seat he's worked for since he was fourteen, you can think again.'

'Please, Kevin,' the ex-junior-minister said, 'could you ask your friend to keep her opinions to herself?'

'We'll see what happens in the ballot,' Kevin said.

Twenty minutes later, the agent entered. 'Would Mr Stuart please go downstairs?' he said. Hamish went out. 'I regret to have to inform you that none of you has been successful,' he said to the others.

'How many ballots?' Kevin asked.

'As you know, it is not customary to reveal details of the voting,' the agent said. 'Mr Stuart has been duly selected and will be presented to a meeting of the whole association in a fortnight's time.'

'It's a Central Office fix,' Kevin's girlfriend said. 'We're not going to put up with it.'

Victor and Belinda ran to his Bentley, which was parked in an alley behind the club. She let him lurch onto the main road before asking what had happened.

'Car accident. He's on a life-support machine. His new girlfriend rang me from the hospital.'

'Ann-Louise?'

'That's it. Ploughed into a lorry. She's all right but the passenger side of the car was a write-off. She said they were being chased.'

'Oh my God.'

Victor was driving extremely fast, but she hardly felt it. He dialled a number on his car telephone. It worked without his needing to hold anything to his ear. A woman answered.

'Vera? Vic here. I'm afraid it's bad news. The boy's had a car accident.'

'How bad?'

'Very bad.'

'So where've they taken him?'

He gave the name of the hospital. 'Intensive care. They say you can't miss it as you drive in.'

'Can we go together?'

'Sorry, I'm half-way there. Don't try to drive. Get a minicab and I'll take care of it.'

Belinda had never been driven so fast.

'Tom's mother,' he said as they pulled out of a roundabout for which he had barely slowed. 'How come, then, he came to be living at your place?'

'I said he could stay, after you'd asked him to leave your flat. We became rather fond of each other.'

'I didn't think you came for the ride.'

'Then he went off with Ann-Louise and Hamish proposed to me instead.'

'So who'd want to chase them?'

'A man called David Cheney who's obsessed with me and thought Tom had behaved unfairly. He's the only one I can think of. The other night I shut the door in his face. I should have tried to stop him.'

'There's no way you can stop someone who's made up his mind.'

She said to herself: 'I pray for Tom. I pray for Tom. I pray for Tom.' Over and over she said it. She had never prayed so sincerely.

They were overtaking a long line of traffic by using the other side of the road. With no room to spare, Victor pulled aside from an oncoming car, drove through a light which had turned to red and pulled away faster still. She did not feel frightened. She wanted him to accelerate. 'I pray for Tom. I pray for Tom. I pray for Tom.'

There was a blockage ahead. 'Hold tight,' he said, and swung off the main road into a street of the half-timbered houses she had described long ago at Mrs Stuart's. She glanced at him. He was enjoying this chance to drive like an idiot. How could he enjoy anything when his son was dying? How could she ever have thought life would be easier with Tom dead? They missed a child on a bicycle and entered a long, flat straight across some drained marshes. She shut her eyes and went on praying.

At the hospital they hurried through casualty and into intensive care. She saw Ann-Louise in the distance, alone outside a partitioned bit of the ward. When they came near, she pointed to a bed half-hidden by curtains.

'They're trying to save him,' she said.

Belinda went forward a few paces, but through the cluster of people and machines could see nothing. Victor came and took her arm. 'We'd better wait back here.' They stood at a loss in the middle of the floor. After a while a nurse noticed them, found out who they were, took them to an adjoining office and asked them to stay there. She disclaimed all knowledge of how Tom was. Later she came and gave them plastic cups of tea.

'I suppose you want to know what happened?' Ann-Louise said. 'We'd left the flat and taken my car when I saw in my mirror that David was following us. He must have been waiting outside the flat for a chance to have a go at Tom. We had a chase. Tom was loving it but David's car was more powerful. I tried to pull across some traffic. That was when we got hit. Afterwards I don't think he knew a thing.'

The hand Belinda gave to Ann-Louise was stiffly accepted, but only for a moment or two.

It was an hour before a doctor came to see them. 'Mr Coleman? I'm afraid we did all we could but your son's injuries were too severe. I know it's no consolation, but if we had saved him he would probably have been paralysed for life.'

A nurse put her head into the room. 'Jerry's on the line for you.'

'I'll take it out there. As I say, I'm sorry, but it wouldn't have done any good to operate. It was a hopeless case.'

'May we see him?' Belinda asked.

'I'll just find sister for you.'

The doctor escaped. They heard him arranging a game

of squash with Jerry. 'It's time I got my revenge,' he said in a cheerful tone.

Nobody came. Victor went to find the sister. He returned and said it would be better if they didn't see Tom. They were making their way down the ward when they met a middle-aged woman with peroxide-blonde hair. 'Vic?' she asked. 'Where is he?' Belinda fainted.

Twenty-Four

One by-election soon blurs in the public mind into another. Hamish's contest was memorable, if at all, for open warfare in the local Conservative association. The Tories' skill at keeping their quarrels private had deserted them. A right-wing faction told the press that Hamish had been railroaded in by a secret alliance between Central Office and a local property developer, who together infiltrated and subverted the otherwise impeccably democratic selection process. The 'missing fiancée' briefly attracted attention, but no pictures of her were available to catch the reader's eye. Most people who saw the story probably accepted the candidate's assurance that far from being imaginary, she was ill. His robust defence won a degree of respect from the reporters covering the campaign, who tried as usual to bring it alive by tearing the candidates to pieces. One journalist described Hamish as 'a heroic mediocrity battling to rebut the allegations of an unattractive group of local racists'.

In the second week, Hamish counter-attacked by drawing attention to the Labour candidate's Trotskyite past and challenging the Labour leadership to repudiate her. Meanwhile a steady stream of ministers came down to his morning press conferences to endorse him. He had enough workers to get his leaflets out, though not to canvass as intensively as he had hoped. Kevin's claque started to seem irrelevant.

Its views were so repellent that if Central Office had interfered, it must have been justified in doing so.

Throughout the campaign, Hamish was dreadfully worried about Belinda. Until it started, he had been able to help look after her in London, but that was impossible once he was working flat out in the constituency. Her mother drove down and took her back to Yorkshire. She was thin, listless, without appetite.

The doctor could find nothing wrong. Mrs Gould and Mrs Stuart agreed that it had all been a great upset, her lodger running off with Ann-Louise and getting killed, and Belinda being pregnant so opting for a quiet wedding once the by-election was over. There was, however, an enormous amount to be said for starting a family. They said it.

Her father sold the picture that was supposed to pay for the wedding. The auctioneers found it had been misattributed and it fetched a derisory sum. 'I never liked looking at it, but at least I had the pleasure of thinking it was valuable,' he said. He made Belinda drink port; was the only person for whom she made an effort to appear better.

At his suggestion, they set out one afternoon on her favourite walk from the house, past the church and into a wooded valley. The last time she had come here, on the weekend Tom left her, she had thought how she would enjoy showing him the place. Today, the lovelier the woods and river looked, the less she could endure it. She saw the way up to the grassy ledge above the path where she had thought that if the weather was fine – it was perfect now – they might lie together. 'Let's go back,' she said.

Every night, Hamish rang to see how she was. 'You must eat for the baby's sake,' he said. 'As soon as this is over we'll marry and go on honeymoon.' She started crying. He wanted to get in his car and drive to her that instant.

The name Tom, and the phrase 'I love you, Tom', came into her head at all hours of the day and night, and she found it hard not to say the words out loud. She was bitter against David, who claimed Ann-Louise's story about being chased was nonsense. Two witnesses could vouch he had been in Northamptonshire on the day of the accident, looking at a hunter. He was shocked to hear of Hamish's new engagement and swore never to speak to him again.

Ann-Louise lost her driving licence, but chose to let the question of David's involvement in the accident drop. She was said to have started an affair with a junior but married partner in her firm. Hamish hoped the rumour was malicious invention.

Belinda would not stay up to hear the result of the by-election. Her mother came in to tell her that Hamish had held the seat by five hundred votes and everyone was saying what a brave and skilful campaign he had fought. 'You'll like being married to an MP,' she said, knowing she would like being mother-in-law to one. MPs were not tremendously well paid, but the allowances were considerable and even today there was some kudos attached to the position. He could get directorships, and employ his wife as his secretary.

Hamish arrived the next morning, having barely slept, and went up to Belinda's room. She was still in bed. Despite her illness she looked adorable.

'I'm sorry I haven't been here,' he said, kneeling down and holding her hand.

'I'm sorry for being the missing fiancée. Well done.'

He bent and kissed her hand. She felt the back of his head.

'I couldn't say this on the telephone,' he said looking up, 'but of course if you don't want to go through with it, you don't have to.'

'Don't you?'

'Of course I do. I found a house we might buy. They say it used to be a farm.'

By the time her son was born, they were putting down roots in a thriving English community. Belinda asked Vera Coleman to be one of the godmothers. Neither Mrs Stuart nor Mrs Gould approves. They note, too, that Belinda has stopped taking trouble over her appearance, but comfort themselves that a marriage has taken place.

The new Mrs Stuart loves her baby and makes Hamish happy. He recently invited the Scott-Woodhouses to dinner. Belinda was relieved to find how little strain they imposed on her, though she had not met them since the night Tom stayed behind. Neither he nor David was mentioned. Matthew wanted to know if there was any wildfowling to be had on that stretch of the Thames estuary.

Driving back to town, he remarked to Jenny that Belinda was losing her looks.

'I suppose she is,' said his wife, who had no looks of her own to lose and was pleased to see things evening up. 'I had a long chat with her while you told Hamish about your jolly old duck flighting. Did you gather what she's doing? Some sort of training to become a social worker! Beat that! She said she knows people like us laugh at social workers, and one or two of them are pretty dire, but she's never done anything half so worthwhile before and feels far happier than when she lived in London. She didn't want to know what the rest of us are up to.'

'It's tragic,' Matthew said. The change in Belinda had shocked him, but he consoled himself with the thought that he had less reason to envy Hamish.

'Men are such babies,' Jenny complained.

If he hadn't been with his wife, Matthew would have talked for a long time about the miracle of Belinda's beauty, which still amazed him when he remembered it; and about his sudden, gloomy realization that they had all become middle-aged.